After a family tragedy, Andy and Emma sell everything they own to buy a rundown inn on an isolated beach on Kauai's south shore. The plan is to rebuild the property and their lives. Will the couple last long enough to see things through? Will they want to?

ALSO BY LEE SILBER

Jimmy and the Kid
The Pelican
The Splendid Splinter
Sunshine
The Homeless Hero
Runaway Best Seller
Summer Stories
Show and Tell Organizing
No Brown M&Ms
The Ripple Effect
Creative Careers
Bored Games
The Wild Idea Club
Rock to Riches
Chicken Soup for the Beach Lover's Soul (Contributor)
Organizing from the Right Side of the Brain
Money Management for the Creative Person
Self-Promotion for the Creative Person
Career Management for the Creative Person
Time Management for the Creative Person
Aim First
Notes, Quotes & Advice
Successful San Diegans
Dating in San Diego

LEE SILBER

HARPER'S BAY

Rebuilding an Inn, and a Life

For my sons, Ethan and Evan.
I'm so proud of you.

–LEE SILBER

*"Sometimes we must break apart completely
in order to rebuild better."*

–ANDY CLARKE

PROLOGUE

"The view from up here is amazing. I can see the entire bay and the water is so clear I can make out the pattern of the reefs. Come on, climb up," Andy yelled down to Ray, the property's original handyman.

"I'm good. I don't do well with heights. Besides, the roof isn't as sturdy as it looks."

"Funny, it doesn't look that sturdy," Andy acknowledged, looking down at the rusted, weather-beaten metal.

"Because it isn't," Ray answered back. He would know, he'd been "maintaining" the abandoned inn for absentee owners through every kind of natural disaster imaginable.

"Man, I can't believe this place is mine. It's so crazy." Andy said to himself as he stared off at the horizon and past the outer reef where the ocean was a darker shade of blue and the water was white-capping from the warm, afternoon trade winds.

Ray heard him and said, "I can. Nobody's lived here since… well, I can't even remember. It was before the Hurricane."

"Lane?"

"No brah, Hurricane Iniki, in 1992."

Andy pondered that and said, "That long?"

"It's not like this is a popular place, or easy to get to," Ray said, sweeping his hand from one side of the expansive property to the other. This included the main house and the three beaten down bungalows in back, the acres of unspoiled land, and the dirt road running through the middle of it all.

"I know, but look at this beach. It's completely empty," Andy observed, but had to admit as he looked out that except for a few small breaks in the reef, the beach was not a safe place to swim and Ray was right, the inn was so tucked away nobody would ever know it was here, unless they accidentally discovered it with a drone.

"Most tourists wouldn't be able to find this place, and if they did they couldn't get to it without a four-wheel drive." Ray, knew his way around since he'd lived on Kauai his entire adult life. He spent his free time exploring the island in his beat up Toyota 4x4 that was so old and rusted it was hard to distinguish the original color.

Andy took one last look around at the miles of unspoiled greenery behind him and the big beautiful bay in front of him. It was a dream come true to call this home

"Ray, I'm coming down. You got a hold of the ladder?"

"Hang on, I'm gonna move it over to the other side, it's a little bit safer," Ray said, looking at the tall man standing on a slippery metal roof sporting a cowboy hat, boots, jeans, and plaid shirt; out of place in the Kauai climate, or to be walking around on a weather-beaten roof.

"Be careful Mr. Clarke."

"I'm good," Andy said, stepping gingerly before putting his full weight on the spot he was going to step next, slowly making his way from the high point of the slanted roof to the edge. "It's a good thing this roof is made of metal," Andy commented, seconds before losing his footing and tumbling off the roof and landing on his back with a sickening thud.

"Harper. Is that you? Son!" Andy reached out and pulled his teenage son in and held him so tight he worried he might squeeze the life right out of him, but he couldn't help it.

He held his son at arm's length, impressed with how his boy had filled out. "Look at you. You're so tall." Andy wrapped his arms around him again. He missed Harper so much, and the tears flowed down his cheeks and he bawled like a baby. Being reunited with his son was all he ever wanted, and here he was.

"Dad, it's okay." Harper said in a reassuring voice.

Everything seemed brighter and warmer than before, like the sun shining through after a drawn-out storm. Andy ran his hand through his son's hair and put his arm around his shoulder. "I love you so much. You know that, right?"

"I know, Dad. I love you, too."

"Why did you leave then?" Andy asked, tears welling up in his eyes again, his curiosity and emotions getting the better of him.

"I'm sorry."

Andy didn't want to ruin the reunion so he simply said, "It's okay, you're here now. That's all that matters. You're here now."

"Yeah, I'm here now."

"I wished for this since the moment you left. The first thing I knew I would do when I saw you again was tell you how proud I am of you and that you're perfect just the way you are. You're everything I ever wanted in a son. Everything I ever wanted in my life. I'm so sorry I didn't tell you all of this before. It's my biggest regret."

"I know, Dad."

"You do?"

"Yeah, I do."

"I can't believe you're here."

"It's beautiful a piece of land, Dad."

"I'm glad you like it because I'm never letting you out of my sight again. Remember that time when you were eight and I couldn't find you at the mall? That feeling of pure panic and dread I felt when I was searching for you was so intense."

"I know."

"I never would have forgiven myself if I hadn't spotted you in the Lego store. I was so relieved, I was overwhelmed with relief and joy when I found you. That's how I feel now. I'm so glad I found you again and that you're okay."

"I'm okay."

Andy started tearing up again. "We had so many good father and son times together, just you and me. Do you remember those days when you were little?"

"I do."

"I cherish those times so much. They were the best years of my life. I wish we could go back and do it all over again."

"You'll always have those memories, Dad. Always."

"Oh my God, your mom! She needs to see you. She really needs to see you. You leaving hit her really hard. She acts like she's okay, but she isn't. She's really not doing so well. The truth is, we're not doing so well. The house in Slidell is gone. Hurricane Ida completely destroyed it, and the dock, and the boat. Everything is gone.

That's why we bought this old inn, your mom and I. Truth be told, it was mostly my idea, but she'll come around. I know it doesn't look like much, but I think by rebuilding it we can rebuild our lives—and having you here to help makes this perfect. A real father and son project. We'll work side by side, taking breaks to swim in the ocean.

Heck, we'll fix up that busted up boat over there and go spear fishing on the outer reef and barbecue our bounty when we get back. After dinner we'll be out on the porch, exhausted and sunburned, but loving life—the three of us sitting around talking, laughing, and sipping ice-cold beers looking at the moonlight dance off the water in the distance."

Harper nodded and smiled, but didn't say anything.

"Did you know I wrote a song for you, 'The Things I Never Said'? Dang it if Jim McDaniel didn't record it and turn it into a number-one hit on the country charts. It was kind of a big deal for a while. It's how we could afford to buy this place."

"I heard it. It's a really good song, Dad. Your best so far."

Andy smiled and said, "Come on, let me show you around and then I'll play it for you and you can sing with me like you used to."

Harper just stood there and smiled. "Come on, let me show the bungalow you can live in. It needs some work, but we can fix it up together." Harper didn't move.

Andy started to feel the same fear he felt when Harper was lost in the mall. He was going to lose him all over again, he just knew it. Harper slowly began fading away and disappeared into a warm, bright light that hurt Andy's eyes.

"Boss, wake up," Ray pleaded, kneeling next to Andy on the ground.

Andy lay perfectly still, the bright tropical sun creating a warm glow inside his eyelids. He kept them closed and searched for his son in his mind. He was gone… again.

"Boss, you okay?" Ray asked, concern etched in his voice and on his face.

Andy opened his eyes. "Harper! Harper, my son was here. Did you see him?"

Ray paused, pulling off his ratty baseball cap and running his fingers through his long, graying hair. "No, I didn't see him. You told me your son died, remember? I'm sorry."

Andy ignored Ray's comments and said, "No, he was just here. Right here. I swear."

"I think we should get you to a hospital."

"No! No hospital, I want to stay here, right here. I need to find Harper."

"On the ground?"

"Yes, just leave me here."

Ray decided he would walk away and call an ambulance when out of earshot of his boss. Clearly Mr. Clarke suffered some sort of head trauma.

When Ray was a few feet away he watched Andy violently begin banging the back of his head against the ground as hard as he could, doing it again and again and calling out Harper's name. After the fifth and final whack he lay still.

CHAPTER 1

Ray stood staring at the inert body on the ground. His new boss was breathing, he checked, but beyond that he didn't know what to do for someone who knocked themselves out. He'd leave it to the paramedics. The Old Koloa Fire Station was a few miles away, but it would still take them a while to arrive, and an ambulance coming all the way from Wilcox Hospital in Lihue would take even longer. He had time, so he walked over to the front steps of the main house and sat down. This way he could keep an eye on his boss and ponder his next move.

It came as quite a surprise when the old owner called to tell him the property was sold. The surprise was that it took so long to sell this valuable piece of paradise. The buildings weren't worth much, but the beachfront parcels were priceless. Over the years the original owners hung onto this prime piece of real estate knowing its value would only increase and they could pass it down to the next generation. They also lived on, and off, the land so it wasn't just an investment, it was home.

The family lived in the main house while other relatives occupied the bungalows. Ray's mother was raised in the main house. Being almost completely isolated from others and home schooled, it was not a happy childhood. Ray's mom couldn't wait to turn eighteen and move away—she didn't wait, she left at age seventeen.

She moved to Oahu and married a soldier. Soon after the young couple had a child, Raimanu (Ray). When the family found out she'd married a Haole (a non-Hawaiian) and had a child, they cut her off and cut her out of the will. Ray grew up on Oahu, never knowing much about his family history. It wasn't until after his parents passed away—his father in a motorcycle accident and his mother from an overdose—that he learned about the land.

At first he would just sit on the beach out front and stare up at the big house. It took him a while to get up the nerve to approach the people who lived there, only to find out it was now an inn that catered to tourists wanting to get away from it all and experience what old Hawaii was like. Hearing that, Ray asked the innkeeper if they were hiring, and that's when he started work as the inn's resident handyman—and he slept in the work shed behind the buildings.

The house was built from the ground up, but the bungalows were bought and transported from an old sugar plantation. None of them were well built, so there was plenty of things to fix—but it was dangerous. For reasons unknown, bad things constantly happened to good people on the property. Eventually the unexplained incidents and accidents drove Ray's relatives to move out and create the inn instead.

Not long after, the same strange happenings spooked the employees and scared off the guests. Hurricane Iniki finished things by doing a lot of damage with a direct hit in 1992. What was left of the dwellings sat empty for five years as the recession drove the price of the property down and the living heirs decided to sell. A buyer from the mainland bought the land as an investment. The new owner couldn't care less about what was left of the main house and bungalows, so Ray was out of a job—until squatters moved in.

The most recent owner had the place cleared out and asked Ray to stay on and keep an eye on things, which turned out to be both a blessing and a curse. Ray's salary was just enough for him to not pursue a career or look for better work, and he lived there rent free. Ray built himself a workshop in an old shipping container once used for storage, and even though there was no running water or electricity, a generator provided the power, and a clever rainwater system generated just enough water for the basics. His bed was a cot in the corner of the space.

Living like he did wasn't exactly healthy. Sure, he ate a lot of fresh-caught fish and grew his own fruits and vegetables, but Ray was a heavy drinker and spent too much time in the sun— and it showed. His ratty, Salvation Army clothes hung from his small and skinny frame (except for a modest beer gut). His long gray-tinged hair was pulled into a pony tail under his frayed and sweat-stained trucker-style hat. Sunglasses disguised the bags under his bloodshot, tired eyes. His wild, a ZZ Top-like beard hid his missing teeth. Scraggly long hair completed the look. He was old enough to order from the seniors side of the Denny's menu, but his diminutive size and fetish for hip, new t-shirts with funny sayings made him appear much younger.

As the siren sounds grew closer Ray knew the Fire Chief would question how yet another person was injured here on the property. The truth was he wouldn't have a good answer. Things like what happened to his new boss happened to himself and others on a regular basis. Maybe it was time to demolish this place and leave it to the spirits that seemed to be trying to drive people away. Or, maybe he could use the ghosts to help him get rid of this unstable new owner from the mainland and have the place to himself again.

CHAPTER 2

The flight attendant in first class gently removed the champagne flute from Emma's hand without waking her. After serving her two gin and tonics before the plane left the ground (plus the refills the passenger poured from her purse), Emma reluctantly switched to champagne, passing out before the plane reached its cruising altitude. The passenger in the window seat gave a shrug and helped the flight attendant with the blanket, covering the softy-snoring traveler as she slept.

In mid-flight Emma awoke suddenly and screamed, "No!" Her outburst startled everyone in first class, especially her unwilling companion seated next to her who had also dozed off. Everyone stared for a moment as Emma covered her eyes, bent over, and started sobbing quietly.

"Are you okay?"

Emma raised her hand, but didn't look up.

"Can I get you anything?"

Again, Emma just raised her hand.

"I don't mean to pry, but whatever it is, we can talk about it."

Emma turned her head and looked over as if seeing the woman next to her for the first time. "Thank you, but you wouldn't understand and I don't want to burden you with my problems."

"It's not a burden, and what better time to talk to someone than on a long flight like this. I'm Luann, but everyone calls me Lu."

"Are you going to Kauai on vacation?" Emma asked, fishing another mini gin bottle out of her purse and quickly downing it.

"I was born on Kauai, but raised on Oahu. Now I live in Las Vegas. So, I guess I'm going home. How about you?"

"It's complicated," Emma said.

"Okay. Let's start with something simple. Where are you staying?"

"I'm at the Grand Hyatt Resort."

"Oh, you're in Poipu. I love that side of the island. I'm staying with my auntie in Kapaa. My brothers and I used to camp where the Hyatt is now when we were kids and jump off the cliff at Makawehi Point, next to Shipwreck Beach."

Emma froze. She couldn't move or speak. She just stared straight ahead, in shock.

Luann put her hand over Emma's and they sat in silence. Luann broke the ice and said, "I hear the hiking trails over the hill and around the corner from the cliffs are still there."

Emma shuddered, and said with a shaky voice, "Then you've probably heard of the Queen Emma Inn."

"Of course. It's that run-down place you come to at the end of the Mahaulepu Trail. I hear it's haunted."

"Yeah, well, I own it."

"You own it?"

"After watching way too much HGTV, my husband had the crazy idea we could renovate the old inn and restore it to its former glory."

"I don't think anyone would ever describe the old inn as glorious."

"I know. That's what I said."

"Wait, didn't you say your name is Emma?"

"Yes, ironic isn't it?"

"I don't know. The real Queen Emma came to Kauai to regain her health and spirit after losing her only son, and then the King a year later. There's a festival in her honor every year."

"I'm aware." Emma downed the little gin bottle and then cracked another one. Seeing this, the flight attendant walked over and politely told her she wasn't allowed to bring her own booze. Emma drained the second bottle dry and handed the empties to her and said, "Sorry," tears running down her cheeks. The flight attendant was taken aback and just turned and walked away.

"I didn't mean to make you cry."

"The only time I don't cry these days is if I'm sleeping or working, which is about all I do anymore."

Not wanting to pry, Luann changed the subject and asked, "What do you do for work?

"I'm an attorney, so I deal with other people's problems all day."

"Huh," Luann said, not sure what to ask next, or how to get Emma to open up and tell her what was making her so emotional and sad.

With the flight attendant keeping an eye on her, Emma asked, "Are you going to drink that?" Pointing to Luann's nearly full glass of wine.

"No. You can have it."

Emma downed it and then put the empty glass back on

Luann's tray. "Thank you."

"Are you sure you're okay?"

"Define okay," Emma stated confidently, used to hiding her drinking from her partners and clients, but ultimately failing.

"Well, will you be able to walk off this plane under your own power or will you need a wheelchair?"

"Fair enough," Emma said, slightly slurring her words. "I'm going through some things and it's not going well, if I'm being honest."

Luann pondered what Emma said and replied, "No matter what it is, I've heard it all. I'm a bartender and cocktail waitress at Caesars Palace."

Even with Emma's high tolerance to alcohol, she was now drunk and more willing to let a stranger peak around the wall she'd built up around her. "My husband is in the hospital," she blurted out.

"Oh my God, is he going to be okay?"

"Oh, yeah. He fell off the roof of the inn and has a mild concussion. With his hard head, he'll be fine. He's probably sitting on the beach drinking a bunch of beers right now."

Luann thought to herself, "What a pair," but said, "Will your husband be staying with you at the Hyatt when he recovers?"

"Oh, hell no. I think he lives in one of the bungalows at the inn. This is his dream and my nightmare," Emma said, then added, "I'm the breadwinner in this family and I plan to make full use of the Hyatt's first-class facilities—the pool, spa, and especially the bar. He can visit if he wants."

"What does your husband do for a living, other than renovate old haunted houses?"

"He's a handyman, I guess, when he chooses to work,

which isn't all that often. Otherwise he's a musician, which was his hobby until he wrote a song about our son..."

Emma choked up and stopped talking. Luann waited a minute, putting two and two together before asking, "Is the song, 'The Things I Never Said' by Jim McDaniel?"

"How did you know?"

"I was just listening to it on my phone. It's one of my favorites, but so sad."

"If I hear it, I just fall apart."

"I understand. I'm so sorry for your loss."

Emma started crying and couldn't stop.

CHAPTER 3

"First time here?" the handsome Hawaiian bellman asked Emma as he helped her from the limo she rented for the ride to the resort.

"I came here with my family last time," Emma replied as she stood and straighten her wrinkled blouse and skirt, working to keep her emotions at bay, but truth be told, it was during her last visit to the island when her life all but ended, but now was not the time to break down and cry. Instead her eyes welled up behind her dark sunglasses and she simply willed herself to keep it together.

"Welcome back," the bellman said and snapped his fingers and the hostess appeared with a Mai Tai on a tray.

"Mahalo," Emma said, glad to have a fresh drink in her hand, thinking this will mix well with the opioids she took before the 30-minute ride over. After checking in and being shown to her ocean-view room, Emma tipped the bellman and proceeded to pass out face first on the bed—before he even had a chance to open the curtains.

"Did you grab my guitar?" Andy asked Ray as he wheeled him out of the hospital. Seeing his brand new custom Sprinter 4x4 van parked out front made him smile. It meant his guitar and a change of clothes were inside. The elaborate van was expensive, but since it served as both his home and transportation, it seemed like a worthwhile splurge. Besides, after years of making just enough money to get by or living off his wife's income, it felt good to walk into a dealership and drive out with something so cool—and not have to ask for anyone's permission.

"Whatta ya think?" Andy asked.

"About them letting you out of the hospital?"

"No. The van."

"I'll say this, if you didn't make it I was going to take off in this thing," Ray said with a laugh.

"I'm glad I pulled through, then." Andy stood up and an orderly took the wheelchair away while Ray opened the passenger door. Andy walked around to the drivers side and got in.

Ray shook his head and said, "You're the boss, Boss. Are we heading home?" Ray asked.

"Yeah, with a slight detour on the way." Andy had other plans.

Ray admitted aloud that he had no idea what Andy was planning, and that he was ready to step in and stop it if it was something crazy, dangerous, or both.

They sat in silence as they drove through the famous tree tunnel on their way into Poipu and the turn off to the Grand Hyatt Resort—which was also a shortcut back to the inn. When Andy turned into the resort's employee parking lot Ray gave him a curious look.

"What?" Andy asked with a shrug of his shoulders. "I've never missed a gig in my life, and I'm not missing one now just because I was in the hospital."

"Do you want to talk about what happened back at the inn?" Ray asked.

"No. I want you to drop me off, park the van, and then come and help me set up."

"Yes, Boss. It's better than being alone at the inn with all the ghosts."

Andy pulled around back, grabbed his guitar and gear, and walked away without a word.

With it being dark and the effects of the drugs and alcohol still swimming around in her system, Emma wasn't quite sure what time it was when she woke up. She thought about ordering room service to get a meal and a bottle of booze, but it would take too long so she pulled her matted hair into a ponytail, quickly freshened up, and headed for the bar. On the way there she checked her phone and saw dozens of work-related e-mails and texts she'd missed on the flight over, the ride in, and during her afternoon nap. There was also a text from Luann. "Just checking in. I hope you made it to your resort okay and if you're up for it, I'd love to meet you for a drink at the hotel bar. Just keep your hands off my wine," which was followed with a laughing emoji.

Emma texted back, "I'm heading there now. Love to meet. I can't promise I won't want a sip from your glass—and when I say sip, I mean the whole damn thing. Come at your own risk," also followed by a laughing emoji.

Emma sat at the first empty bar stool upon entering Stevenson's from the lobby. Behind the back end of the big bar Andy was setting up. Both had no idea either was there.

CHAPTER 4

Emma waved Luann over, a drink already waiting for her—or possibly a backup for Emma. Before sitting down at the bar Luann stopped and said, "The guy performing tonight is really good."

"Is he? I wasn't really paying attention. Here, I ordered you a glass of wine. I'm so glad you made it."

"Isn't this place the best? It's like an old library or someone's study in a mansion. Look at all the koa wood, and the art on the walls," Luann said, looking around.

Emma didn't say anything, she was frozen in place, mesmerized by something off in the distance. "What is it?" Luann asked noticing tears running down Emma's cheeks. Emma opened her mouth but nothing came out. Luann looked around and then realized what was happening. The singer was performing the song "The Things I Never Said." It wasn't Jim McDaniel's version, it was better. When it was over, the whole place stood and cheered. Emma put her head in her hands and wept.

Sitting around a cocktail table just off the stage Emma, Luann, Ray, and Andy shared a drink and some small talk.

"I didn't think you would be released from the hospital so soon," Emma slurred.

"The hospital didn't want to release him, Mr. Clarke kinda insisted and they finally gave in just to get rid of him," Ray chimed in.

"I know what that's like," Emma quipped.

"I loved your song," Luann said to break the tension.

"Thank you. I love what Jim McDaniel did with it, but how I played it is how I first heard it in my head."

"Did it take you a long time to write?" Luann asked.

"Not at all. I didn't really write it."

Ray looked at him and scrunched up his face like he was confused.

"The song kinda just came through me. The song wrote itself, literally."

Emma had heard all this before and for all the money and fame it brought, she would trade it all in a second for Harper to come back. After the song dropped other country stars asked Andy to write for them, but nothing he wrote was as good as "The Things I Never Said." Andy's heart just wasn't in it, but he was still paid handsomely for his work.

"Are you coming to the inn tomorrow?" Andy asked Emma, surprised she would choose *this* hotel for her stay..

"I don't have a car."

"I do. I can pick you up."

"No, I don't think so. I really just came here to make sure you're okay. You seem okay, so maybe I'll stay by the pool tomorrow and then head home after that."

"I understand," Andy said. He really didn't, but he also didn't want to push it, so he changed the subject.

"Hey Ray, I was thinking tomorrow we would start by doing some demo work on bungalow three and then go into town and get some supplies to start rebuilding it so you have a proper place to live."

Ray's mouth literally dropped. "You want to work on one of the bungalows so I can live in it?"

"Of course. Sleeping in the tool shed is no way to live. I saw your air mattress in there."

"Yeah, well, the bungalows aren't exactly safe."

"So let's make them safe, starting with yours. We'll begin bright and early tomorrow."

Andy got up, grabbed his guitar, tipped his cowboy hat and said, "Ladies," and walked away. Ray chugged the last of his beer and followed.

As promised, Andy woke up bright and early and headed over to the tool shed with two cups and a thermos full of coffee in hand, excited to begin working on the inn, and grateful to have someone to help him.

Andy lightly tapped on the door of the shed to wake Ray up so they could begin planning what they would do first. "Ray, it's Andy. You ready to go?"

Andy looked at his watch, it was 7:00 a.m. He knocked again, and again there was no reply. Disappointed, Andy sat on a folding chair in front of Ray's makeshift home and poured himself a cup of coffee. He let his mind wander and allowed himself to feel good for the first time in a long time. It felt good to play live music in front of people again. It felt good to see his wife again. It felt good to begin a big project with a lot of potential—and put on his tool belt again and build something special.

Yet, he knew at any moment a sound, sight, or smell would remind him that he'd lost his one and only son. On any given day, he would be triggered to tears a dozen different times. It was the life of a grieving parent—a constant tug trying to drag you down a swirling torrent of grief. If you let it, it would suck you down to a dark place. To keep his head above water, Andy did what he could to keep busy.

It was already a warm day and getting warmer by the minute. Andy looked at his watch again and decided he should change out of jeans and into shorts, even though it was demo day. He poured out what was left of his coffee and got up to head back to his van to change, more than a little disappointed Ray wasn't awake.

Ray came bouncing down the dirt road that led to the Inn, a cloud of red dirt following his truck. Ray opened the rusty, squeaky door and popped out.

"Hey boss. I woke up early and picked up breakfast at Little Fish. You know, the colorful little coffee shop down the road. Here, I got you the Hippie Bagel sandwich."

"Thanks, I think."

"I realized I don't really know you yet, so I went with something I thought you'd like."

Andy unwrapped the bagel sandwich and saw the hummus and sprouts and wished it was bacon and eggs, but he was touched that Ray woke up early enough to go get breakfast, so he simply said, "Thanks. Now let's see what kind of tools we have to work with."

Ray opened the tool shed and Andy knew right away they would be making a trip to the hardware store after breakfast.

As the day grew long, Andy looked at Ray and he was covered head to toe in dust and dragging. The two were physically drained and done for the day after gutting most of the bungalow.

"Boss, I haven't worked this hard, well, ever. I have to admit, it feels good."

"I know what you mean. You did good today, Ray. You really know how to swing that sledgehammer. It probably weighs as much as you do."

"Yeah, and you're pretty dangerous with a sawzall. Maybe we should have switched tools."

"I'm gonna take a shower to get all this dust off," Ray said. Meaning he was going to hold a hose over his head.

"I'm going to jump in the ocean."

"Okay, be careful. The reef is really sharp."

Andy trudged off toward the deserted beach in front of the property and made his way to the small space in the reef he remembered seeing when standing on the roof. With nobody around, Andy stripped down to his boxers, waded in and swam through the cutout in the reef. The warm, clear water felt fantastic. He made his way past the inner reef to a light blue patch where the sand bottom made it possible to stand. Heaven… and it got better.

Walking down the beach was a beautiful woman dressed in hiking gear straight out of an L.L. Bean catalog—khaki shorts, a white top, tan vest, and backpack. It took a minute to realize this woman with her hair pulled back in a ponytail traversing the trail leading to the beach was Emma. She looked stunning.

Sitting side by side on the beach, Andy in his underwear and Emma dressed to the nines, the two took turns sipping from a Yeti water bottle filled with vodka and Gatorade.

"I'm surprised you used Gatorade as a mixer," Andy said, trying not to sound judgmental.

"A girl has to stay hydrated, right?"

Andy raised the water bottle as a one-sided toast and took a big gulp.

Emma took the Yeti back and refilled it from a bottle of vodka stored in her backpack cooler.

"It's beautiful here, don't you think?" Andy asked.

Emma looked around and said, "Yes Andy, it's beautiful. But it's not my dream, it's yours."

"I understand. What does that mean for us?"

"I don't know."

They sat in silence as the sun slowly set to the west bringing an end to the warm summer day.

"Are you still heading home tomorrow?" Andy asked.

"That depends."

"On what?"

"If you want me to stay."

Andy turned and faced Emma. "Of course I want you to stay. I want us to create something together that honors our son. I want to change the name of the inn to Harper's Bay. We'll hang his pictures in the lobby and his art in the rooms. We'll be able to keep him close and tell our guests all about our beautiful boy."

Andy didn't let Emma talk for fear she still may say she was leaving. "I also think that rebuilding the inn will bring us closer together. We can get back to where we were, before…"

Emma stared out at the last of the light and said, "Okay, count me in."

They embraced in the sand, hugging and kissing.

"Yuk," Ray said, wiping his mouth and rolling off Andy as

he came back to life. "What the hell?"

Andy was on the ground looking up at the sky. "What happened? Where's Emma?"

Ray put his hand on Andy's chest and said, "Stay down. You were hit by a falling piece of wood and it knocked you out. Another weird one, boss."

Andy closed his eyes and tried to remember, but he had no recollection of it. He did remember sitting on the beach with Emma. His head hurt and he felt around and found the lump on the top of his head.

"That's two concussions in two days, boss."

"How long was I out for?"

"Not that long, but this time it didn't seem like you were breathing so I was about to give you mouth-to-mouth when you started trying to kiss me."

"I thought you were Emma. Sorry about that."

"It's all good, but I'm worried about you."

Andy sat up and looked around. "Did we even get any work done today?"

"Oh yeah, we got a ton of demo done before you went down."

"Help me up." Ray helped Andy get to his feet.

"You good?"

"Yeah, I'm good. I'm going to shower off and head to the Hyatt. I have to talk to Emma."

"You want me to drive you?

"No, I'll be fine."

Andy drove toward the Hyatt Resort, he saw his dream as a message. He had to get to Emma before she left and convince her to stay. He drove as fast as he could considering the rough terrain in a van full of supplies. He was living with so many regrets, Andy knew if he didn't get to Emma before she left and convince her to stay, he could add another one to the long list.

Andy sped down the long Hyatt driveway and braked hard at the entryway to the resort. He left the engine running and the door open as he ran inside, the valet yelling at him as he raced by making a beeline for the front desk, empty except for the lone employee behind the beautiful koa wood counter.

"I'm looking for my wife, is she still here?"

"What's her name?"

"Emma. Emily Parker," Andy wondered if she still used their shared last name or if she'd gone back to her maiden name while the front desk clerk typed away at her keyboard.

"I'm sorry, Emily Parker checked out earlier today."

Andy's shoulders sagged and his head dropped. He fought hard to not cry at the news that Emma was gone and his chance to tell her face to face that he needed her in his life was gone, too.

He mumbled, "Mahalo" and trudged off toward the atrium overlooking the ocean just off the lobby. He was overwhelmed by sadness and a sickening feeling of being alone. He now regretted everything—buying the property, moving to Kauai, and not fighting harder for his marriage. He had run away and as everyone told him, a change of scenery could be good, but wherever you go your problems follow you. They were right.

Lost in his thoughts, Andy almost plowed over the manager of Stevenson's library who was looking down at his phone on his way to work.

"Andy! You were fantastic last night. Everyone loved you. When can you come back and play?"

Andy looked at him with red eyes and a foggy brain and

said, "I, uh, don't know."

"Anytime you want to play, I'll find a slot for you. See you around Andy."

Andy nodded, and walked back to where he left his van before he got the bad news.

"Do you remember helping this woman with her bags?" he asked the bellman, showing him a picture of Emma from his phone.

"Yeah, brah. She got the party started a little early today, if you know what I mean."

Andy knew exactly what he meant. Emma's drinking was never a problem until the death of their son. It became her way of handling the loss and on most days she was gone by mid-morning, but still made a valiant effort to get her work done despite barely being able to walk. Working remotely allowed her to get away with it—or so she thought.

"What time did she leave for the airport?" Andy asked.

"She didn't ask to go to the airport," the bellman said as he hustled to help a group of guests arriving in a rented Jeep.

"Wait, she didn't request a ride to the airport? Where did she want to go?"

The bellman pointed in the opposite direction of where the inn was located and more importantly, not the way to the airport.

CHAPTER 5

Ray sat on the brand new front deck of the newly refurbished bungalow and looked out at the bay before him. It was beautiful—always had been—but now he would have to share it with outsiders. Tourists. Mainlanders. Haoles. The thought of it made him hang his head in despair. As proud as he was of the work he did rebuilding this broken down bungalow so far, he wondered if he was digging his own grave. Was he fixing up what Andy called "his place" so that someone else could rent it by the week while he was exiled to a rented room in town?

Ray shook the thought off and took a long pull from his beer. Maybe Andy was who he said he was, a good guy with good intentions and a broken heart who wanted to build something to honor his son. All he did was buy all of the supplies, spend the past two weeks busting his butt rebuilding the bungalow while also giving Ray a crash course in carpentry, plumbing, and electrical. After long days in the hot sun the two sat and shared beers by the bungalow talking about the work they'd done and the work they would do next. It was Ray's favorite time. Living here alone for so long was like solitary confinement, and messed with your head. Having someone to talk to was nice.

Usually after the fifth or sixth beer Andy would open up and share stories about his life. When Ray asked about his son or his wife, or what led him to Hawaii—and this spot in particular—Andy always changed the subject. Clearly they were more co-workers than friends—and that's what worried him.

As often happened in this part of the island the wind suddenly picked up and howled through the trees. Strange sounds could be heard off in the distance. It gave Ray the chills. By now he was used to the sudden weather fluctuations and strange happenings at the abandoned inn, but it still made him antsy and put him on edge. It was worse when he was alone. With Andy here now the two of them could acknowledge the haunting sounds and cold breezes, but also ignore them and soldier on with their work. If Andy was shook up by what he saw and heard (and what he felt) he didn't let on. Ray was used to feeling like he was being watched and visited here so it didn't bother him like it did when he first arrived.

The things that once brought Andy joy were now simply distractions from the reality that his only son was gone and his wife was nowhere to be found. He held it together, but sitting on the beautiful beach in front of the property he owned, his Taylor guitar in his lap, and a cold beer in his hand didn't mean that much to him. Looking out at the ocean before him, he contemplated swimming out past the outer reef and never coming back. The pull to see his son again was so strong it made death a viable option.

Working on building something to honor Harper was the only thing keeping him going. Everyday felt like summer and he was young again—covered in sawdust, his skin tight from his deep workman's tan, and his body exhausted from building things. This made him as happy as he would allow himself to be.

Andy finished his beer, picked up the empties, and trudged through the sand to make his list of supplies for the morning run to the lumber yard and hardware store. Ray didn't know that part of Andy's morning routine was breakfast at Dani's in town. This local cafe opened at 5:00 AM and Andy was becoming somewhat of a regular. The coffee was average, the food was unspectacular, but the people who dined there were classic. Nobody really talked to him (yet) but just being there made him feel like a local, and it felt good.

Emma held her wide brimmed hat against the wind, clutching tightly to her beach bag filled with the essentials for a day at the pool—pills, pinot, and her phone. She felt badly about making such a scene when she arrived at Poipu Sands without a reservation and demanding a ground floor room with a view… and an early check-in. She got what she wanted, but she didn't win any friends at the front desk in the process.

The first thing she had to do was call her office and clear her schedule, she was going to be in Kauai longer than expected. What would happen next was undetermined, but she was in no condition to handle legal matters or appear in court for her clients, so calling in "sick" seemed like the right move. Everyone would understand. Her next call was to Luann to see if she wanted to have lunch.

She was avoiding the elephant in the room—Andy and the inn. Now that she was staying and literally just a few doors down from the Hyatt, and a short drive or a (very) long walk to the property she half owned, it made it a lot easier if she decided to see her husband and help him realize his dream.

Luann wasn't able to meet Emma for lunch but suggested breakfast in town the next day. Luann was on vacation so there was no need to meet too early, but she was so eager to ask Emma for a favor she didn't want to wait another minute and suggested they meet bright and early at Dani's the next day.

Andy was up at the crack of dawn but didn't wake Ray until the reasonable hour of 7:00 a.m. He wanted Ray to come along for this supply run since they would be choosing fixtures for the bungalow that would become Ray's residence. The plan was to grab a bite to eat and then head over to Home Depot. For Andy, today would be a late start, but he wanted Ray to have a say in how his home looked and he also thought walking into Dani's with a local's local might boost his standing in the community.

Andy and Ray stood and stared at the permanently closed sign, stunned to see that a place like this could close after 40 years. Ray shared with him some stories of coming here in his younger years for the daily special which was all he could afford. The two were about to turn and leave when up walked Emma and Luann.

"Hi Andy. Surprised to see me?" Emma asked and did a quick curtsy in her colorful sundress.

"Surprised, and pleased," Andy said while pulling Emma close for a long hug. He whispered, "Are you here to stay?"

"That's the plan. I want to see this through so I took a leave of absence from the firm and I'm staying at Poipu Sands, not far from the inn."

Luann asked, "Did I hear you right, you're staying on the island to help rebuild and restore the inn?"

Standing in the empty parking lot of the now-closed diner Emma looked at Andy, Ray, and Luann and said, "Yes, for now this is home."

Ray was the first to speak, "Are you handy Emma? What I mean is, are you going to be able to help with the construction?"

Everyone looked at Emma, eagerly awaiting her answer. "I'm better at the design aspect and dealing with the permitting process, but I don't mind getting my hands dirty."

"Ray and I were heading over to Home Depot to pick out a few things for Ray's bungalow, you two want to tag along and give us some ideas of what to get?" Andy asked. "It's right around the corner, by Costco."

"How about we get some breakfast first?" Luann asked.

Everyone shrugged in unison and then looked at Luann for a suggestion. "Why don't you let me cook for you? My Auntie's place isn't that far and I know the fridge is stocked because I just stocked it."

"Sounds good," Ray said right away since he was starving. Emma and Andy both agreed and it was settled, breakfast would be at Luann's.

After an amazing breakfast done local style, Andy asked Luann where she learned to cook.

"I'm self-taught, but I also learned a lot from watching my makuahine a me ka makua, my mom and dad," Luann said and then hung her head.

"Do your parents still live here," Ray asked. "I might know them."

"No, they both died when I was young and my Auntie

raised me," Luann answered.

"I know how that is, I'm sorry," Ray said.

To lighten the mood Andy said, "The pancakes were out of this world and the way you made the omelettes with local fruits and vegetables was delicious. Maybe you could help create a menu when the time comes and we open the inn."

"Of course, I'm happy to help in any way I can. You know, I'm not just a good cook, I also have several other skills that could be useful."

Emma looked at Luann and said, "Are you saying what I think you're saying?"

"I don't want to go back to Las Vegas. I want to stay here and help you guys get your inn up and running. A project like this is just what I need and I'm hoping I'm just what you need."

Emma looked at Andy, and as so many couple do, she communicated with her eyes what she wanted. Andy telegraphed his approval without saying a word. "We would love that, Luann. Welcome to the team," Andy said.

"Call me Lu, and mahalo, I am so grateful."

Ray welcomed Luann to the crew. He was also calculating how this might change his standing in the project. In just one morning the team had doubled in size. "Are you two going to help pick out fixtures at the hardware store?" Ray wanted to know.

"Sure, that actually sounds like fun," Emma said, and squeezed Luann's arm.

Ray hid his disappointment and decided to go with the flow. "Awesome."

"Let me help you clean up this mess," Andy said and began picking up plates.

CHAPTER 6

Instead of going to Home Depot with Andy and Ray, Emma and Luann told Ray it was his bungalow and he should choose what he wanted in the way of fixtures—but they wanted to be sure to reserve the right to help him pick out the furniture when the time came.

Instead, the two new friends were going shopping for clothes since neither had anything that would be considered construction wear. They bought overalls, boots, and bandanas and Andy made sure to grab gloves, protective glasses, and hard hats for the new crew.

Meeting back at the inn, the women looked over everything in the trailer Andy towed behind his van and smiled and nodded in approval.

Dressed in their brand new outfits they announced their presence as they stepped into Ray's half-finished bungalow. Andy had completed the electrical and plumbing and taught Ray how to hang drywall. New windows were installed and the flooring was in, but it was covered with protection paper. It looked and smelled new.

"You like?" Andy asked, clearly proud of his handiwork.

Luann spoke first while taking it all in. "Are you kidding

me? I'd love to live here someday."

"Good, then the next bungalow we remodel will be yours," Andy stated.

"Oh my gosh, I don't know what to say."

"Say you'll help us move some of the cabinets in from the trailer.

"Yes, boss," Luann said, and grabbed Emma by the arms. She wanted to jump up and down, but she guessed Emma was just a little too prim and proper for that, so she just smiled like a child who just got her first bike.

"Let me help you, neighbor," Ray said, and the two went outside.

Emma had tears in her eyes.

"Andy, it's not often but sometimes I allow myself to feel good about things. This is one of those times. Thank you."

"I know what you mean. I think helping others like Ray and Lu helps ease some of the pain. I know it's what Harper would have wanted us to do if he were here," Andy said with tears in his eyes. "Sometimes I feel like he is here, you know?"

"I want to feel that, too. I need that, Andy. You have your song to him and you're building this inn to honor him."

Andy corrected her, "We're building this inn together."

As hard as the foursome worked the first day together, it became obvious they would need more help to complete the larger plans and projects. What slowed them down was the time it took Andy to teach the three non-builders each of the trades that needed to be done. They were all eager to learn, but to pass inspections and keep everything up to code, Andy decided he would hire help as needed, but it wasn't like he could just use Angie's List—or could he?

The good news was Ray could now sleep, shower, and start cooking in his bungalow. The bad news was he would be sleeping on the floor, bathing in cold water, and using a microwave oven. A new water heater, appliances, and furniture were the next step. Still, it was progress.

To celebrate, the four decided to go out to eat and Luann was able to get them a table at Keoki's. The women went to clean up and change at Emma's hotel while Andy and Ray stayed on property and improvised their transformation from being covered in dust and dirt to respectable and restaurant ready.

Keoki's Paradise was a short drive from both the inn and Poipu Sands, and yet it was the perfect escape. From the moment Andy walked inside he felt the aloha. It was the feeling he wanted to create at the inn. It looked, felt, and even smelled like Hawaii. Lush foliage and flowers, cascading water running throughout, and wood and lava rock completed the look. In a word, it was paradise, and it was perfect.

What was unexpected was the band set up by the bar. The sound was definitely island-inspired with a little bit of reggae mixed in, complimented by the beautiful harmonies provided by the backup singers. Andy was mesmerized, then surprised. On ukulele and vocals was the Manager of Stevenson's Library. After the set ended he walked over.

"Surprised?"

"Yeah. I mean, I didn't know you played," Andy said. "You sound great!"

"Mahalo. I'm lucky they let me be in their band. This group is one of the best on the island. I'm just sitting in. Hey, you want to come up and play your song?"

"What? No. I'm sure they don't know it."

"Yeah, they do. It's part of their set. They kind of have their own take on it."

"Am I getting royalties then," Andy joked.

"Uh, that's a no. But I'm sure they would love to have you join in. Come on."

Andy felt his body move in that direction, but he was completely unsure of himself and what to expect. Instead, they greeted him like a superstar, handed him a guitar, and quickly went over their arrangement of his song. It was too cool.

"Hey everybody, we have a real treat for you tonight. You know this song as a Jim McDaniel hit, but the man who wrote it is right here on stage with us and he's gonna join in. For the lucky Keoki's crowd tonight, here's 'The Things I Wish I Said' featuring Andy Clarke."

It was a surreal experience. His song, which he must have played over a thousand times felt new and fresh. Andy loved this Hawaiian-style version. He also had to admit, he loved the way the crowd sang along to the chorus and gave him a standing ovation at the end. What would have made it more special was if Harper was here with him. Andy wondered if Harper was watching, or helping even as good things happened for Andy. He kept his sunglasses on to hide his tears, but in many ways these were tears of joy.

"Thank you everyone. If you could raise a glass to Jim McDaniel for making this song a hit and to my son Harper, who I miss every minute of every day…" Andy didn't finish the toast, but the audience cheered and patted him on the back as he made his way over to Ray and the entrance.

"You crushed it boss," Ray said.

"Thank you, Ray. That was something, huh?"

Emma and Luann walked in looking stunning and said, "Sorry we're late."

"No problem, you two look beautiful tonight" Andy said, and he meant it on both counts.

"Wow, that band sounds incredible," Emma said as she did a little sway from side to side to the groove.

"Yeah, they're really good," Andy replied, not feeling the need to mention his cameo performance a few minutes earlier.

The hostess took them to a table in the middle of the indoor oasis and as Andy looked around he knew he'd made the right decision to come to Hawaii. It felt right, and now with Emma by his side, it was perfect.

CHAPTER 7

"That can't be right," Ray said to himself after listening to the weather report on ISLAND 98.9, his go-to station for island-style reggae. The disc jockey was warning residents of an approaching hurricane. Not since Hurricane Iniki devastated Kauai (and more specifically the south side of the island where the inn was located) in 1992 has a major hurricane hit. Like most locals, Ray blew off the warning and didn't mention it to Andy or Emma. It wasn't due to come ashore until later in the week (if at all) so why worry?

Walking around Ray's nearly completed bungalow made Andy smile. All that was left to do was decorate and fine-tune some of the systems and settings and the place would be move-in ready. Emma and Luann went into town to pick up some towels and linens and Ray tagged along with the women to make sure they didn't buy anything too frilly. He didn't do frilly.

Andy was tempted to hang up his tool belt for the day and go for a swim but he was so close to completing the first part of his plan he didn't want to put it off. So he put on all the door-knobs, adjusted the water pressure, and then went outside to label the circuits on the breaker box. It was tedious and tiring because he would have to flip one switch and then go back inside to make sure that breaker did what he thought it should, and go back out and note it next to the switch in the box. It wasn't until he flipped the last switch that he got the shock of his life.

Andy was alone in a tiny one-person sailboat in the middle of the bay in front of the inn and there wasn't a wisp of wind so he stretched out and looked up at the bright blue sky. Proud of the fact he'd made this abandoned boat float, he closed his eyes and let his mind drift to happier times when Harper was a baby.

All Andy wanted to do back then was hold him in his arms. The two sat in the rocking chair he built, Harper all swaddled up and Andy in his pajamas with his feet up on the ottoman. He talked to Harper about this and that, sang to him, and often just stared at him. It was a bond and a love he'd never known before, or since. Emma called him the baby whisperer because Harper would just look up at Andy with his big blue eyes and quietly listen to his soothing voice. That stage of Harper's life seemed like it lasted longer than it did.

Before he knew it Harper was a toddler with no brothers or sisters to play with so Andy made himself into the perfect playmate and the two did everything together—father and son playdates. Every stage of Harper's life was the best time of Andy's life.

Laying on his back on the bottom of the small sailboat was suddenly making Andy very uncomfortable. His muscles were spasming and he felt a tingling in his fingers. He tried to take a deep breath but it hurt to breathe and his heart was racing at a mile a minute. Andy struggled to open his eyes and when he did a stinging wind forced him to close them again. Suddenly the boat was rocking back and forth, rain pounded his face, and a roaring wind hurt his ears. Andy curled up into a small ball to try and ride out the raging storm. Andy wondered, is this it? Is this how I die?

CHAPTER 8

Andy could hear someone talking, but he didn't recognize the voice so he kept his eyes closed and just listened.

"Your husband is one lucky guy. If you hadn't found him and called for help right away I doubt he would have made it," the doctor stated.

"Does this mean he's going to be okay?" Emma asked, standing by his side.

"He'll be fine, but we want to keep him here one more night for observation. I gave him something for the pain and we treated the burn. His heartbeat is back to normal. When he comes to we'll know more."

"Doctor, why was he all curled up like a baby when we found him?"

"It's how our muscles and tissue react to the shock. It's normal."

"Thank you, Doctor."

After the doctor left the room Andy opened his eyes and saw Emma with her head in her hands.

"Hey, I'm fine."

"Andy! Oh thank God you're okay. What happened?"

"I don't know, I was checking the breaker box one last time

and when I flipped the last switch. I, I, I actually don't remember what happened."

"You don't remember anything?

"Well, while I was unconscious I think I had another vision."

"Did you see Harper?"

"Not exactly. I just had very vivid memories of him when he was really young. I was in a sailboat and all of a sudden I was adrift in the middle of a terrible storm."

"Like a hurricane?"

"Yeah, I guess. Yeah, it was like a hurricane."

"That's weird, because while you were unconscious it was announced that a hurricane is heading for the islands. They think by the time it reaches landfall it will lose some of its strength and only be a tropical storm—but a severe one. Ray and Luann are back at the property putting everything away and preparing the bungalow for whatever comes our way."

"I want to help."

"No, absolutely not. After they finish boarding up and battening down the hatches they're coming here because the hospital is the safest place to be in a storm like this. I just hope they remember to bring food."

Andy laughed, and it hurt.

Luann and Ray raced through the front door as the storm raged behind them. Palm trees contorted with the 70 mph winds—at the top end of a tropical storm and just below a cyclone. The flags in front of the hospital were long gone but the halyards loudly banged against the poles. The horizontal rain hit them hard in the face as the two fought the gusts that wanted to blow them to the ground or worse, carry them away. The noise was intense, like a freight train passing by. The overhang to the hospital entrance did little to help and the doors were locked shut. They tried to yell ideas at each other but it was too loud. Ray signaled for Luann to follow him around to the emergency room entrance which was unlocked. They struggled with the door and an orderly ran over and helped them inside.

"What's it like out there?" he asked.

"I was here when Hurricane Iniki hit," Ray said while huffing and puffing, "It was a lot like this. There's stuff all over, brah."

Luann caught her breath and asked, "Are we safe in here?

"As safe as a person can be in a storm like this. We have a backup generator for our backup generator, so we're good, yeah."

"My Auntie has a landline. I think they work even when the power is down. Do you mind if I use your phone?"

"No problem. Here. I'll get you an outside line."

After a dozen rings Luann hung up. "I hope she made it to a shelter."

Ray asked the orderly, "We're here to see Andy Clarke, he's a patient here. Electrocution."

"I'd normally tell you it's after visiting hours, but you can go on up. He's on the second floor, first room on your left. Take the stairs."

The minute the two walked into Andy's room they noticed he was up and talking.

"You okay, boss?" Ray asked.

"I'm fine. I'm just not sure how the whole thing happened," Andy replied.

Ray just shrugged his shoulders. "Maybe the electricity in

the air from the approaching storm caused it."

Andy knew that wasn't it, but he just nodded and considered himself lucky to be alive.

Emma, always the practical one (except when she was drinking) asked, "Were you two able to get everything important put away?"

"We did the best we could," Luann said. "We put everything in the old shipping container. That thing is the strongest and heaviest thing on the property. If that's not a safe place, nowhere is."

"Thank you both. That was very brave of you."

"What about my van?" Andy asked.

"Don't worry, we tucked it away where the covered bus stop is. It's built like a fort. It was the best we could do under the circumstances," Luann said.

Throughout the night the lights flickered and the skeleton crew of nurses brought cots and candles and assured everyone the generators would hold and the hospital would, too. They were right on both counts.

CHAPTER 9

Watching the news from the hospital room made it clear it would be a while before they would be able to gain access to the inn—which was hard to reach on a good day. Instead, Ray drove Luann to check on her Aunt. She would stay there and Ray would sleep in the van for a couple of days.

Emma and Andy checked into a hotel near the hospital. It was built from brick and designed to withstand a storm like this (something Andy made note of) and came through in good shape—plus they had a restaurant on property which was open for business. The couple took a room with two queen beds.

"Andy, my phone is working," Emma yelled out from the bathroom.

Andy looked down and had one bar, which was one bar more than he had on his phone yesterday. "I'm good," Andy started to say, but Emma in her excitement rushed out in her bra and panties—something Andy hadn't seen in a long time.

"What are you staring at?" Emma asked, apparently forgetting the two were more close friends than a couple now.

"You're beautiful, you know that?" Andy said.

Emma smiled, and said, "Did you hear me, we have cell service."

"I heard you," Andy said. "I was just a little distracted by the sight of your half-naked body."

"Get used to it," Emma said with a smile and turned and went back to the bathroom.

The first call Andy returned was to Jim McDaniel who had called several times, probably worried about how Andy was after the storm. He picked up on the first ring.

"Andy, you're not taking my calls now?"

"What? No. I mean I'm on Kauai and we just had us a Louisiana-like storm roll through here and it wiped out almost all of the dang cell towers." Andy always seemed to slide back into his Southern twang when talking to Jim—Andy grew up in a small beach town on the gulf coast of Texas before moving to Louisiana in middle school.

"Well I've been trying to get a hold of ya all for a coupla' of days now. I got good news. You sittin' down?"

"Matter of fact, I am."

"Good. Ready for this? Your song is gonna be in a feature film starring yours truly. I mean if you're okay with that."

"I'll have to ask my lawyer, she's in the bathroom right now, but it sounds good to me."

"Play hardball with them buddy because the song is a key element in the film. You should get paid well. I know I am. Oh, and by the way, I'm the executive producer of the soundtrack, so don't worry, I got your back."

"I don't know what to say."

"Say yes. I'll have my people e-mail your people the details. Oh, and they want to use one of your other songs, too."

"This all sounds amazing. Thanks, Tim. I appreciate everything you've done for me and my family."

"Andy, that's what friends are for."

Andy put the phone down and wondered, is this Harper's way of helping him achieve his dream? Instead of celebrating this latest development, he cried because he would trade it all to have his son back.

When Emma hung up the phone after closing the deal to have two of Andy's songs on the soundtrack for Jim McDaniel's new film she stood up and took a few paces toward the window and stared out for a long time.

Andy patiently waited a while and then said, "So, what did they say?"

"They accepted our counteroffer without a fight. We now have enough money to hire a crew to help rebuild the inn."

"That's great, so why do you look so perplexed?"

"Jim talked us up so much and told them about how the storm may have wiped the inn off the map that Warner Brothers also wants to do a reality TV show about us while we rebuild and reopen the inn."

Andy let that sink in. "Say that again."

"Okay. First, the agreement to have your songs on the movie soundtracks is a done deal if you agree to three of Tim's stipulations."

"Here we go," Andy said and wiped his brow.

"Just wait. First, he wants you to play at his annual music festival. It's a charity event that raises money for Little Leagues and attracts over ten thousand people."

"Okay."

"He also wants you to play in the celebrity softball game that precedes the event, but he was adamant you have to play for the other team because he said you suck at softball."

"Now that's just not nice—or true. He knows I played high school baseball and two years in college."

"It was a community college," Emma said.

"You, too?"

"I think he was kidding about what team you would be on."

"All right, that's two stipulations, what's the third?"

"He wants you to join him on some tour dates after you go to Nashville and record some of your songs."

"I always knew Jim had a big heart, but this is above and beyond."

"Well, I should mention a lot of this would be done in partnership with his production company, so if we succeed he succeeds."

"I don't have a problem with that, do you?"

"No, I do not," Emma said and sat on Andy's lap. "I'm so proud of you. I always believed in you, even when you doubted yourself."

Andy looked at Emma and then he kissed her and they and embraced—both had tears in their eyes.

Emma stood up and wiped away her tears, "I'll call them back to tell them we have a deal and to send me the paperwork."

"There's not a better lawyer on this island to handle this," Andy said.

Emma corrected him, "There's not a better lawyer west of the Mississippi to handle this."

Andy didn't disagree.

Once again Luann made the foursome a big breakfast at her Aunt's house, which wasn't easy with the power out, but she managed by only opening the fridge once and triple checking that nothing had spoiled—and she was pretty sure Spam never went bad.

Emma explained to Luann and Ray exactly what had transpired since they were all together at the hospital.

Over lukewarm coffee it was Ray who spoke first, "So, we would become reality TV stars."

Luann hit him on the back of the head and said, "That's not the point. The point is the inn will be built in a fraction of the time it would have taken the four of us, even with several subcontractors helping. Plus, when the show airs, it will provide most of the promotion we'll need to get guests to come to Kauai and stay with us. It's a blessing, Ray."

"And I'll be famous," Ray said, half joking while Luann raised her hand to fake hit him again making Ray flinch.

"The only thing for certain is we have more money to spend to hire a crew which means we can focus on our strengths and keep Andy out of harms way," Emma noted.

Everyone agreed. "If you want, I can represent you guys," meaning Luann and Ray, "and make sure your contracts are fair."

"We get paid." Luann stated, but it was more like a question.

"I did a little research, it's not a lot, but yes, we would all get paid. Plus, Andy and I will start paying you a salary as well, so you two don't have to worry about money and can focus on this project."

"It's been three days since the storm and it's been sunny two of those days, I'm thinking we can make it through in the van."

"What are we waiting for then, let's go see how much of the demo work nature did for us," Andy said, and then asked Ray for the key to his van.

CHAPTER 10

On the bumpy ride in Ray couldn't believe how much damage the storm did to the trees. Almost all the leaves were ripped off and the trunks were all bent over in the same direction. There was all kinds of debris strewn about and a few random loose items that seemed way out of place—like a surfboard impaled on a branch high up in a tree. Some spots were still flooded, and several of the old or flimsy structures didn't make it through the storm. It was surreal.

Selfishly, Ray wondered what the storm did to his brand new bungalow. It seemed like a cruel trick to have just finished it and then have to start over and rebuild it again—if Andy was even willing to do that. If worse came to worse he could go back to living in the workshop. It wasn't that bad. Plus he would have the whole property to himself if the Clarke's abandoned ship and left. His gut told him Andy was in it for the long haul which meant there was now going to be contractors and a camera crew around every corner.

Luann sat in silence, seeing her island damaged like this was heartbreaking. She was also worried about her Auntie who was staying with a friend on the other side of the island. Her house made it through, but the gallery where she worked was all boarded up because a tree fell through the roof. Maybe Andy and Emma could hire her to help, too? Her aunt was an artist in her own right and had an eye for design. She would wait a while and bring up the subject when the time was right.

Luann also was counting her blessings. Being part of a project like this beat the heck out of living in Las Vegas and working in a smoke-filled casino. She truly liked Emma and Andy. She wasn't yet sure about Ray, but he hadn't done anything to make her *not* like him, still...

Whatever they found when they got to the inn, she was ready to tackle head on—no complaints. She wasn't afraid of hard work and she would show them every opportunity she got.

Emma reached over and touched Andy's arm. No matter what they found, they have been through worse. She knew she pushed Andy away when the truth was he was hurting just as much as she was and right now he needed her support. She couldn't go back and change what happened or how she handled things, but she could make an effort to support Andy's dream— which, if she was being honest, was now her dream as well.

She would assess the damage and then decide if she was up to making this her full time job. At first she thought maybe she would fly in and help out when she could, and the reality show contract would allow for that, but what she really wanted to do was roll up her sleeves and go all in. She loved the law, but the long hours, demanding deadlines, and difficult (and often dishonest) clients took a lot of the joy out of her job. Quitting the firm wouldn't be hard, it would be more like removing a box of bricks from her back.

Andy couldn't keep the smile off his face—and then it hit him. What if all this good fortune was the Universe's way of giving him everything he ever wanted and then ripping the rug out from under him… again. Now he was fearful of what was waiting around the corner—both literally and figuratively.

When a storm even worse than this one destroyed their last home, Andy and Emma decided to just walk away. Insurance covered most of the loss, but they both wanted to get away from the place with so many memories. It was odd that lightning would strike twice, but in retrospect it was possibly the best thing that could have happened—this time and last.

Andy was excited to show the new plans to everyone. They weren't totally up to spec and would need to be redrawn by a real architect, but he'd put his vision for Harper's Inn on paper while laid up in the hospital and using his decent drafting skills (and thanks to the nurses going to Walmart to buy him some supplies) the dream came to life. Nobody knew this, but the more damage done by the storm the better. It would mean less demo and less work in the end since saving the old structure would be harder than simply rebuilding it with more modern methods and materials. His new plan was based on a total re-build with more cleared land to work with which made the old professional plans obsolete.

Andy also wanted to take a closer look at the breaker box to see why he had been electrocuted the way he was. It didn't make sense. He wired the thing himself.

As the van turned the corner from one damaged dirt road to the entryway to the inn it was clear the severity of the storm was greater than expected, and its path ran right through the property.

Andy parked where the four wheeler once was—it was flipped over at least a football field away and the winds ripped the trees out by their roots just for fun and tossed them aside. Everyone got out to take it all in. The damage done to the old structure was unbelievable. It was as if a giant came and pulled the roof off and tossed it aside, stomped on the old bungalows—except for Ray's rebuilt and reinforced structure which was still standing.

There would be no way of knowing what caused the short that nearly killed him because the outdoor breaker box was hit by debris and broken—and yet Andy jumped for joy. "Oh man, this is awesome!" Andy said, bouncing around from one pile of wood and debris to the next.

"I think your husband has lost it," Luann said to Emma.

"Oh, he's crazy. But in this instance he's crazy smart because he listened to me for once and took out an insurance policy on everything you see that's destroyed. It was expensive, but now it will pay off."

"My brand new bungalow is okay," Ray announced with tears of joy in his eyes.

Emma walked over to Ray and stood by his side and surveyed what little was left of the structures they'd purchased with what was (at the time) the last of their money. She was also savvy enough to know the land and location is where the true value lies—not to mention the beach—and the old buildings were falling apart anyway. Plus, the insurance settlement would come in handy as they rebuilt everything. Would they ever get insured again? Unlikely, but they were just taking it one disaster at a time these days.

She didn't have the heart to tell Ray that the plan was to start over from scratch and that the bungalow would be torn down as some point in the process. With a tractor or two everything could be cleaned up and cleared out and they could start with a fresh slate.

The fact that her and Andy's relationship was in the same predicament—they'd both went through a terrible storm and now they needed to rebuild their life together. The history would still be there, but both the inn and their lives could be better than before.

CHAPTER 11

"Hey Trudy, did you get the memo? We're going to Hawaii," Tex Tillerson announced to his co-producer, Trudy Thomas, and then did a quick hula motion.

"Oh great, you want me to celebrate spending the next year-and-a-half in a mosquito infested, deserted part of Kauai? I can't wait," Trudy sarcastically replied. She then flipped him the bird.

"Did you see the aerial pictures from the drone? It's raw and beautiful. The shots will frame themselves."

"If you say so," Trudy answered, secretly agreeing that the location was picturesque. "If I have to do this I want to stay on the civilized side of the island. I hear the Princeville Resort is nice—and it rains all the time. A couple of the crew stayed there when they filmed scenes for a Harrison Ford movie."

"How old are these guys?"

"Old enough to know they don't want to stay in a hurri-cane-ravaged dump of a bed and breakfast on the side of the island a storm recently ripped apart," Trudy pointed out.

"They're building an inn, but I hear ya. There's a perfectly good hotel a few miles away. It's a Hyatt and I think the crew will appreciate the proximity to the location of the shoot and the property's many amenities. We'll all jump off the cliff next to the property and call it a team building exercise," Tex joked.

"Count me out. I don't do cliffs, I'm scared of the ocean, I hate beaches, and I'm a redhead from Surrey, England—I don't do sun."

"Perfect."

"You can be such a wanker, Tex. Is Tex even your real name?"

"No, but it makes things easier when people think I'm from Texas. It kinda sets the tone."

"Are you even *from* Texas?"

"No, but people assume I am. See?"

"I don't see. Why would you want people to think you're from Texas?"

Tex just shook his head. "Have you looked at the files on the cast. It's reality TV gold."

"I haven't seen the files because I'm trying to get out of doing this bloody project."

"When you hear this I think you'll change your mind, suck it up, and buy a case of insect repellant and sunscreen because this is gonna be good."

"Does this dodgy show even have a name?" Trudy asked.

"The name came from Jim McDaniel, and it's brilliant. Ready? Okay, here it is: *Made Inn Hawaii*. It's perfect, right? Made *Inn* Hawaii. Get it?"

"Yeah, I get it. It's clever and catchy, I'll give you that. What else you got, mate?"

"Let's start with the two main characters. Their marriage is hanging on by a thread after they tragically lost their son."

"How did he die?"

"He jumped off a cliff and never surfaced."

"Were the parents there?"

"They were nearby when it happened."

"Okay, that's tragic. What else?" Trudy acknowledged.

"The mom, Emma, is an attorney and a raging alcoholic. If we play our cards right, and with a little nudge, we can get her to go over the edge."

"A little, '*Housewives of Kauai*' action," Trudy said, nodding along with the plan.

"Yeah, something like that. The isolation will help because we can corner her in her worst possible moment and get her to open up on camera."

"I like the way you think. Cruel, but creative. What else ya got?"

"The husband was a loser handyman who hit the jackpot when he wrote his version of 'Tears in Heaven,'" Tex pointed out.

"I'm not following," Trudy said, and meant it.

"Remember when Eric Clapton's kid fell from the 53rd floor of a New York City apartment and died and then he wrote that sad song about it? I think he even won a Grammy."

"Vaguely."

"Well, our boy did the same thing. 'The Things I Wished I Said' was written by Andy Clarke, a wanna-be country star who works construction. So cliché, right?"

"I have to admit, I love that song. Call me sappy, but it makes me tear up whenever I hear it. I didn't know the backstory. Wow. We can absolutely use it. Plus, our boy is a musician. We can do a scene with him around a campfire while we roast marshmallows and sing, Kumbaya."

"You're both sappy and cynical at the same time."

"I'm complicated."

"Well the good news is Jim McDaniel and his family are planning to surprise the couple when the project is done and be the first ones to stay there. Who else can say they have that ace in the hole for their show?"

"Right. Now we have the two them playing guitars around the campfire."

"Better yet, they are going to do an intimate concert on the grounds."

"How intimate?"

"A hundred people. Mostly the people who will help build the place and if I have my way, a few more who can win a trip and a chance to see Jim McDaniel and Lizzy McDaniel in concert as we promote the show in advance."

"And Andy Clarke."

"Yeah, him, too."

"You said Andy and his wife are on shaky ground. Can we use that?"

"I think we can drive a wedge between them and see what happens, but I'm hoping they stay together. That's just me," Tex added.

"Now who's sappy? Who else is part of the cast?"

"Let's see, we have the caretaker, Ray Raimanu."

"Do they call him Ray Ray?"

"It's not noted here, but we can insist, especially if he hates it."

"What's his story?" Trudy asked, always playing the angles.

"Okay get this. His family once owned the old inn and the surrounding property, but they sold it because they claim the place is haunted and they wanted out. In today's dollars it would be worth tens of millions, but he was cut out of the will and his relatives sold it and after it changed hands a couple of times before Andy bought the whole thing on the cheap and now Ray just works there—for Andy," Tex said, reading from a thick folder of advance research.

"He has got to be bitter about the whole thing," Trudy said in a wishful way.

"Exactly. We can leverage his arrests and the fact he's suspected of using the property as a place to grow weed which he sells on the side."

"Are you kidding me? You couldn't script this."

"Maybe. But wait, it gets better."

"I can't wait to hear what's coming up on our next episode of, *As The World Turns, Hawaiian Style*."

"Luann, who is known as 'Lu Lu' back in Vegas where she works as a cocktail waitress, is deep in debt to some dangerous people. Apparently she has a pretty serious gambling problem."

"This home improvement show is becoming so much more. I love it."

"Tell me more about the wife, Emma Clarke," Trudy asked. "I think she could turn out to be the star of the show.

"Well, she's an attorney with a large firm in Baton Rouge," Tex said as he read from a sheet in his file, but he knew the juicy details by heart.

"Is Baton Rouge the capital of Louisiana or is it New Orleans? I can't remember," Trudy asked.

"Baton Rouge is the capital, but she lives—or should I say, lived—in Slidell, about an hour-and-a-half away. After a hurricane destroyed their home, Andy stayed there to help rebuild the town and Emma rented an apartment near her office—an hour-and-a-half drive away."

"Were they separated?"

"Not officially, but we suspect she may have been seeing someone," Tex added.

"Maybe we let it slip that she's possibly having an affair with a co-worker—it doesn't even have to be true, the accusation alone would be enough to get Andy all riled up," Trudy said with a devious smirk on her face.

"Like I said, I'm pulling for them, but the show comes first. Always," Tex assured her, but even he was taken aback by Trudy's willingness to manipulate the narrative and possibly destroy lives all for better ratings.

"Right. I have an idea. Do they have their own general contractor? Maybe we could bring a hunky one from the mainland and have him try to seduce her."

"Don't forget in the end this is a home improvement show," Tex reminded her, "and between the drama we have to make sure they can work together and finish the project."

"The pending visit from the McDaniels will be the pressure the show needs to push them to meet impossible deadlines, and the crew of tradesmen we'll bring with us can do a lot of the heavy lifting."

"I think Andy wanted to hire local talent," Tex noted. "That's what I would do."

"The more the merrier," Trudy said and walked away, a definite skip in her step."

CHAPTER 12

Andy spread his hand-drawn plans out on a makeshift table (which was basically a piece of plywood balanced on a pair of orange Home Depot buckets, with the plans held in place by four rocks) in front of Ray's bungalow which was left where it was, for now.

To better visualize the plans they stood in the middle of the clearing they'd created after the storm using rented equipment—no small feat when everyone else on the island wanted and needed the same equipment, but Andy overpaid and said when he was done he would help out anyone who needed it free of charge. It was worth every penny to watch Ray, Emma, and Luann take to the task like (semi) pros after some basic instruction. Now they could see what space they had to work with, and it was a lot more than before.

Andy left the cover on the plans while they waited for the newest member of the team to arrive so nobody could sneak a peek.

Around the corner came a beautifully restored vintage VW Camper Van in mint green with white accents. It was the version with small windows all the way around. Very rare, and very cool. The woman behind the wheel parked and slowly got out. She was a big woman, but beautiful in every sense of the word. She seemed to glide as she approached in her floral muumuu dress, her radiant smile and the hibiscus in her hair projected warmth, but a tilt of her head and a glance from her brown eyes let you know she was a serious woman. She walked straight up to Luann and kissed her on both cheeks.

"Everyone, this is Lily, my auntie." Everyone said hello and Luann continued on. "She's going to be helping us and she brings a lot to the team. She's lived here her whole life and is immersed in Hawaiian culture. She's also well connected and can help us get the local help we'll need."

Emma continued, "Lily will help us design and decorate the property and make sure we don't do anything to dishonor the heritage of this sacred land."

Andy added, "These plans are only a first draft of what's possible for this place. I value all of your input to help make it great for locals and tourists alike."

Ray spoke next, "I appreciate that. As you know, my family owned this land and but I wasn't a part of the decisions about what it was used for. I'm stoked I can now have a say now. Mahalo, bruddah."

"Of course, Ray. Okay, with that said, here's what I was thinking," Andy proudly announced while removing the cover sheet from his preliminary plans for Harper's Bay Inn and Retreat.

As everyone perused the plans nobody spoke, they were all clearly blown away, but questions were also quickly forming, which Andy sensed and said, "Before I explain what you're looking at," he handed everyone a pencil. "Feel free to pencil in anything you think of that will make this the special place Emma and I know it can be."

"Before I begin, there's a couple of things I want you all to know. The first one is the main house and the bungalows will stay true to their original design—there'll just be more of them and everything will be bigger and more spread out. Ray, we'll move yours if you want or you can choose one of the new ones. The second thing is even though we're adding a lot of new amenities, we will have a high employee-to-guest ratio so we can take care of all of our guests needs and hire as many locals as we can—which is why you will see a lot of back-of-the-house buildings—including living quarters."

"Last, but not least, Emma and I have decided what we want the inn to be about."

Emma choked on her words, then began. "As you all know, we lost our son, Harper, which is why we came up with the name, Harper's Bay Inn and Retreat. We want to focus making this a retreat for people dealing with grief."

Luann put her hand on Emma's shoulder and Ray fist-bumped Andy.

"With that in mind, here's what we have so far," Andy said and then added, "Remember, there are no bad ideas, so if you think of something that will improve the plans, speak up."

For the next thirty minutes Andy and Emma proudly talked about all the cool things they wanted to build, which included: the new and improved two-story main house with it's open-air design, wrap around lanai, and unobstructed view of the ocean.

Next to the main house was a small restaurant in which guests could have their meals. By the beach would be a bar and grill area and next to it a tiny coffee shop that also served ice cream—something Harper loved. Something else their son would have been a fan of was the game room built as a tree fort;

a little retreat for kids and teens.

Some of the other structures for the guests included bungalows to house a small spa, a mini movie theater, a boutique, and a gym. By the bay, a water sports structure would be built that would include dive and snorkel gear, stand up paddle boards, and fishing gear. Other structures included a large gazebo-covered area off to the side surrounded by a large lawn area that could be used for yoga, meditation, workshops, and maybe even weddings.

Placed even more remotely, and at the end of a winding path through foliage was a round, stand alone structure made of lava rock, driftwood, and other organic elements. The building looked like a refined version of a hut you'd find in Tahiti, and it sat on a small hill with steps leading up to the entrance. This was the grief center. Inside the round room were hundreds of little drawers. Each one would be for a person who had passed. Guests and locals alike could put whatever they wanted in the drawer designated to their lost loved one and label it themselves. In the middle would be a place to sit and record a message to your loved one. The Grief Center would also be accessible from a public hiking trail that would run through the property.

A short distance away was another structure in the same style, but this one was to be a Heritage Center. In it would be an attendant who could point out the native flora, wildlife, and artifacts hikers might find on the trail. It would also serve as a cultural center where kids could come and learn about Hawaiian history. In addition, fruit trees would be planted around the site and water would be available for hikers to enjoy.

When guests first turn off the service road and onto the

smaller one that led to the property the goal was to line it with plants and trees so when you arrived at the entrance it opened up to feature a large sign and reception area letting you know you've made it to paradise.

Most of the buildings for staff-related stuff was hidden by tall trees and lush landscaping. This included a workshop, laundry room, storage facility, and a water reclamation system (inspired by Ray's original idea, but this one was in the form of a tower with his family's name painted on it to honor the history of the property.) Also, as a nod to the way Ray lived off the land was a large garden and greenhouse to grow vegetables and herbs, fruit trees, and a chicken coop. There was space for several generators, charging stations for the golf carts and electric vehicles, and an office for housekeeping and other services. Separate, but close was a staff chill area with hammocks, a barbecue, and tiki bar—but the staff and their families were welcome to use any of the amenities on their off days.

Luann, Lily, and Ray stood around speechless while staring at the elaborate plans. Ray broke the silence first. "This is insane, bruddah. You've outdone yourself. I just have two questions. The first is, whatta ya think about getting a Zodiac with a small outboard engine. I know a cut-through in the reef and we could take guests out there to snorkel?"

"Love it, Ray. Emma, can we do that?"

"Sure, I'll just need to write up a waiver and we're good."

"What was your other question?"

"Where am I gonna live?"

"Right. Sorry. See these villas on the other side of the property, out of view of the guests, but on the beach? That's for all of us. Or, we can move your current bungalow over."

"No, I love the new villas. Can we build those first?"

"Of course, neighbor, but you bring up a good point. It's going to take a while to get this all approved."

"It's new construction now, not a rebuild," Emma pointed out. "We'll need to hire an architect and then get the permits before we can do anything."

"I know where to find a good architect," Lily said. "I'm not sure how their offices faired during the storm, but there's a firm near the gallery in Old Koloa and they specialized in adaptive reuse and historical renovation services. From what I hear, they're the best on this side of the island."

"Let's set up a meeting," Emma said.

"I think they can coordinate the whole project from the ground up," Lily added.

"Even better because Emma and I are going back to the mainland for a while so after we get the official blueprints and permits pulled we'll let the show know we're ready to go," Andy said. "But in the meantime I have to go to Nashville and Emma is going back to Louisiana."

"I should probably go back to Vegas, pack up my stuff, and quit my job," Luann said.

"I guess I'll stay here," Ray said.

"I was hoping you would say that," Andy said. "As usual we need you to keep an eye on things."

"Alright Lily, we're ready for you to bless this land," Andy said.

Lily began performing an ancient ritual and almost on cue and true to form the wind suddenly kicked up and knocked the makeshift table over, tore the plans for the inn in half, ripped her ceremonial headrest off and carried it toward the mountains.

Ray looked at Andy and raised an eyebrow as if to say, see what I mean about spirits and strange things happening around here.

As if on cue, clouds quickly formed and a squall had every-one running for cover.

CHAPTER 13

Over the next two months it was a lot of hurry up and wait. Andy and Emma met with several architects and ended up going back and choosing the first one they saw and the one Lily recommended. While the architect worked on the plans and permits, everyone but Ray and Lily left the island. Lily visited the property as much as possible and helped Ray get in touch with his Hawaiian heritage. Ray was back to living like he was before, only this time in a custom bungalow, with a brand new company truck to get around, and a nice paycheck deposited in his bank account every two weeks. With nothing to do but show surveyors around or clean up this or that, Ray started having parties of one in his bungalow, sometimes beginning in the middle of the morning.

Luann wanted to do the right thing and give her employer two-week notice that she was quitting and leaving Las Vegas. She also wanted to end her lease and not leave her landlord in the lurch. It was the right thing to do, it was also the dangerous thing to do. Her plan was to tell her employer she would work the midnight shift in the casino where there was little chance she would bump into anyone who knew her. She cut and colored her hair just in case. She went to her apartment to pack up in the off hours as well, parking around the corner and entering from the backside of the building. She was very careful, and for two weeks it worked. Luann wanted to collect her last paycheck and get her security deposit back to pay for her trip back to Kauai. She almost pulled it off, but when she was tipped off that her bookie was looking for her she left everything behind. Not a good look, but she did what she had to. Luann sold her car, bought a first-class, one-way plane ticket and headed home to Hawaii, never looking back.

Andy was on cloud nine. During the day he recorded in one of the nicest studios in Nashville and with the best musicians he'd ever played with. His songs came to life and based on what everyone heard, they felt he had an album's worth of material. Thanks to Jim McDaniel's help, Andy Clarke was going to be a recording artist in his own right. Writing and recording helped him better deal with the loss of his son, but in other ways it brought up a lot of raw and painful emotions. He cried a lot, but in the end the songs were sensational—and a couple were even upbeat and hopeful. He honored his son in song and started to try and lead to a life without Harper, one with meaning and purpose—helping others navigate through their grief. He couldn't wait to get back and start building the inn.

When Jim went on tour he brought Andy with him to sing "The Things I Wished I Said" as a duet, and Jim let Andy sing and play one of his new songs on his own. Andy's life was never in a better place and still a wave of sadness and loss would overwhelm him at least once a day and sometimes bring him to his knees. As wonderful as things were, there was an emptiness in it. Many times he wished he could share the moment with his son. Other times he was just trying to fill up the hole that ran through his life. Everywhere were reminders of what was and what will never be—commercials, movies, music, and seeing other fathers with their sons. It hurt like nothing he'd ever experienced, but after each performance the line of people wanting to talk to him grew larger and longer. Grieving parents came to hear him sing and sought him out after shows to personally thank him for his songs. This, more than anything else, helped him heal.

Emma returned to the law office she was still technically employed by, but instead of working on past cases and clients (which she passed off) she focused on setting up the business side of running an inn. With all that happened already, she made sure to cover any and all contingencies that could occur. Emma was in her element and the work took her mind off her grief—except at night, which is when she slipped back into some of her bad habits. Emma also worried the money they had in the bank and what was coming in wasn't going to be enough to cover the costs of building everything Andy envisioned. Instead of taking a loan and incurring new debt, she had an idea.

CHAPTER 14

"You must be Ray. We've heard so much about you," Trudy Thomas said, while holding her hat down with one hand against the island breeze and her other hand clutching the two-way radio she was known to scream into.

"Do I know you?" Ray asked, not sure who this obvious mainlander with an English accent was, but she looked like Indiana Jones if he had rust-colored, shoulder-length hair and stood five feet tall with boots on.

"I'm so terribly sorry, I'm Trudy Thomas, I'll be producing *Made Inn Hawaii*."

"Oh," was all Ray could muster. He was a little buzzed on beer and didn't remember being told the producer was coming to visit today. If he had he may have skipped the last two cans of OMG Hazy IPA—which was how he felt.

"Are you the only one here?" Trudy asked, looking around as she lit a cigarette and pulled an inch-thick sheath of papers from her oversized leather shoulder satchel and handed him them to Ray. "This is your contract, sign and initial it where it's marked and get it back to me today."

Ray hesitantly took the contract and asked, "Shouldn't I have a lawyer or someone look at this?"

"You did," Trudy said and exhaled a considerable cloud of smoke in Ray's direction.

"I did?" Ray replied, not sure he actually had.

"Emma reviewed all the contracts. She's a barrister, no?"

"A barrister?"

"A lawyer."

"Yes. Yes."

"So we're good to go then, right?"

"Uhhhh, yeah, sure. Just wondering," Ray said while flipping through the papers as he spoke, "how much do we get paid?"

"You get a base salary of $1,000 a week," Trudy said, already bored with Ray and ready to move on. "So, are we here alone?"

"Well, I'm alone, but it looks like you have a whole crew with you."

"You're a funny one, eh? Good. Good. We can work with that."

"Um, back to the pay. Is there a stipend or food allowance?" Ray asked.

"Normally craft services feed the cast and crew. I heard we're supposed to only use local food trucks and serve Hawaiian plate lunches, I hear they're sort of like bangers and mash."

"Uh huh, I see, and Emma said $1,000 a week is enough?"

More impatient than ever, Trudy replied, "That's what you, Lu Lu, and Ditzy get."

"You mean Luann and Lily? What about Andy and Emma?" Ray asked.

"Everyone gets the same, Ray. Everyone."

"Even you?"

"No, I make a whopping $2,500 a week."

"Ohhhh," Ray said, both shocked and embarrassed. I thought it would be more."

"Didn't we all. Didn't we all," Trudy said finishing her smoke and flicking it into the bushes.

Ray wondering what Lily would do to Trudy if she saw her doing that. "So we'll be seeing a lot of one another?" Ray asked, not sure if he was hitting on her or just confirming a fact.

"Not if I can help it." Trudy said under her breath.

Curious, Ray asked what a reality television producer does.

"What don't I do?" Trudy answered, while walking away with Ray in tow. "I do everything from concept to casting, contracts to counseling, and I create a story that is told over a series of weeks. I also have to manage the money, the personalities, and the pace of production so that we don't end up with a shit show."

"Do you mean a shit show as in a show that sucks, or a shit show meaning things on set are chaotic, contentious, and get us canceled."

Trudy turned around, tipped her sunglasses down slightly and looked over the frame, "You're not as dumb as you seem. I like it. We can use that."

Ray took his hat off and did a semi bow and said, "At your service." People always underestimated him. Always. He was no dummy, but nobody needed to know that. Nobody noticed he read a new book every other day and had for years. Books kept him company while he was out here alone. Ray knew a little about a lot of different things—including reality television production—but it was better to just listen and learn than let on he wasn't the dullest tool in the work shed.

Trudy called the crew over and instructed them to start filming whatever they saw that looked interesting. She wanted stock footage of island life she could pull from later. Tex called and Trudy stepped away from Ray and the crew to answer.

After a few minutes she was back and said, "Ray, come with me. There's something I'm going to need your help with."

CHAPTER 15

"Laissez les bon temps rouler," Jim McDaniel called to Andy as he ran on stage as the opening act for the first time on the last date of the tour.

"Let the good times roll," Andy answered back, showing that he knew what his fellow Cajun was saying. The two had become very close on the road and in addition to giving him his big break, the McDaniels continued to help him in ways he never expected. The couple's charity, Neighborhood Helper, which provides humanitarian services in the event of a natural disaster, sent money and supplies to the residents of Kauai after the storm and made sure the gift was on behalf of Andy and Emma. Jim and Lizzy also promised to come to Kauai and do a benefit concert in the future.

Andy performed his new material with Jim McDaniel's band backing him with the plan to close with "The Things I Wished I Said" and Jim coming out to sing with him, instead of the other way around as they'd performed it throughout the tour. This would be the first time Andy introduced the song—to 15,000 strangers. He *could* just play it without any explanation, but he'd been pushing himself musically and personally while on the road—Andy learned all of the songs in the set and stayed on stage as an extra guitarist backing up McDaniel from start to finish—so he took a deep breath and went for it.

"Thank you for helping make one of my dreams come true—to perform my original songs in front of a crowd like this," Andy said and put his hands together as if praying and bowed his head. The crowd erupted with applause.

"I know you're all here for the most accomplished country star on the planet, so I'll close my set with a song I wrote, but he made famous." The crowd cheered loudly.

"Getting to know Jim on tour has made me love him even more. He's just as nice in person as he is onstage. He's good people, as we say in the South." More cheering.

"Before I bring him out I want to tell you a little about this next song. My son Harper was my everything. I never thought I could love something or someone as much as I loved him. I was so proud of who he was and what he'd done. I meant to tell him, but…" Andy paused as tears streamed down his face. The cameraman captured the emotion as Andy appeared on the big screen. "We lost Harper before I could tell him the things I meant to say."

Andy took a deep breath, looked to the sky and said, "This song is for you, son. I love you." There wasn't a dry eye in the house.

CHAPTER 16

"Andy, I wanted to run an idea by you," Emma said on the phone from Louisiana. "I approached the Board of Land and Natural Management to see if they were interested in acquiring some of our property for their conservation program."

"When you say acquire, do you mean purchase the land from us?" Andy asked.

"Yes, purchase. They have grants and donations and they want to save large swaths of land for cultural and environmental reasons. This would give us extra working capital and guarantee some giant hotel isn't built behind us. Plus, it's the right thing to do. They love what we're doing—our mission, the low-level structures, and the extensive planting of native plants. They already own a lot of the land next to ours and around it and they want to connect it all up."

"Would people still have access to the property?"

"Yes. They want to protect the land from future development and preserve the way Hawaii used to be. We agree to keep our beachfront footprint as small as possible and build the Hawaiian Heritage Center, but construct it on what will now be their land."

"Sounds like a win-win."

"It is. I'll draw up the papers and get the ball rolling."

"Ray called and said the show sent some people to scout the construction site. How are we doing with that last permit we need to break ground?"

"We just got it so everything's a go."

"Perfect timing then with the tour ending," Andy pointed out.

"I'm so happy for you, Andy," Emma said.

"You mean you're happy for us. Without the music, none of this would be possible. As fun as it was, I'm so over the road. I can't wait to get back to Kauai."

"I bet you had a lot of fans while you were on tour. Female fans."

"Ha. It was a family affair. Did you know that Jim and Lizzy are never apart for more than three days?"

"I did *not* know that. We've been apart for three months, but it seems like longer."

"I know. I miss you."

"I'll see you in a few days, then," Emma said, and hung up. Not sure why she didn't say she missed Andy, too. Then again, she had her reasons.

CHAPTER 17

Andy, Emma, Ray, Luann, and Lily stayed connected with what started out as weekly updates via videoconferencing. As time passed the group chats became less frequent and eventually, unless it was of vital importance, the group didn't communicate at all. Andy and Emma conferred with the architect, project manager, estimator, and each other. Lily and Luann lived together and they would check on Ray from time to time. Otherwise, everyone was busy living separate lives.

Now that construction and filming was about to begin and everyone was on the island, Andy invited the group to meet for breakfast at Kalapaki Joe's, a mostly local place in Poipu that was far enough away from the property and the production team they could talk in private about what's been going on and what would happen next.

After hugs and high fives, the group grabbed a booth in the back (the whole place felt like a treehouse) and ordered. Andy filled everyone in on a few things he knew that nobody else did until now. The first tidbit was the news that Jim McDaniel sent someone undercover from his production company to be his eyes and ears on set. Her name was Christy and she renovated homes on the side so she should be able to hold her own as part of the work crew.

"I also hired someone I know and trust from the mainland to work with the local project manager and who won't be distracted by the lights and cameras," Andy said. "Bradley is a no nonsense guy who will make sure the work gets done."

"Emma, you want to tell them about the latest developments on your end?" Emma pulled the contracts out of her shoulder bag and passed them around. She explained the terms to everyone and made them aware of what they were signing, assuring them she found and fixed anything that was a potential pitfall.

"I also have some good news. We sold the surrounding land back to Kauai to be used as a nature preserve. The proceeds will come in quite handy as the expenses start to add up. And Lily, they loved your idea for a cultural center and we want you to oversee that aspect of the project."

"Of course. I'm so happy that the land is back in the hands of the people of Kauai and that we can educate everyone who visits about the history of this great place," Lily said with hands to her heart.

"The rest of us will stick together and work as a team on projects around the property," Andy announced. "I saw how hard you worked during the demo phase, so I have no doubt we'll get the job done. Ray, Luann, anything new with you? Anything you want to add? Emma? Lily?"

Each person shook their head no, and dug into their breakfast. Andy wasn't the only one with secrets to reveal, Emma, Luann, Lily, and Ray all knew things the others didn't, but for now were keeping quiet.

CHAPTER 18

It was quickly clear that there were two job sites. The first was the crew doing the heavy lifting under the watchful eye of Bradley, Andy's right-hand man who quickly won over the local workers with his firm, but fair approach and incredible knowledge of the process and the trades. They had the big equipment and were doing big things. The camera crew would occasionally get shots of them in action, but the bulk of the filming was taking place elsewhere with Trudy directing things and Tex whispering suggestions in her ear.

"Andy, I want you and Ray working on building the bar by the beach. Emma and Luann, come with me," Trudy shouted out.

Andy shrugged his shoulders, looked at the plans and the pile of materials and got to work. Ray tagged along as usual, but it was almost like he was reading from a script when he spoke.

"Are we gonna have to encase you in bubble wrap for your own safety, boss?" Ray joked awkwardly.

"I'm not worried," Andy replied, "I have an angel looking out for me."

Ray was caught off guard by Andy's answer, maybe expecting him to say something else, but he played along. "Oh yeah, who might that be?"

Andy put his saw down, looked up at Ray and tilted his head, but said nothing. He wasn't sure what to make of this made-for-TV version of Ray.

"Ray, you know who I'm talking about."

"Hey boss, I decided I want to be known as Ray Ray from now on. Okay?"

"Whatever," Andy said and shook his head.

"So… Harper. How did he die?"

Andy unclipped his leather tool belt and dropped it on the ground and turned his trucker-style baseball hat around and got right in Ray's face, sort of. Andy was almost a foot taller. "What did you say?"

The camera crew stayed back, but they were rolling and getting into position to film a fight.

"I just asked how your son died. What's the big deal?" Ray said as he backed up toward the sand, waiting for Andy to charge.

Instead Andy reached out and grabbed Ray by the throat and said, "I don't know what you're playing at, but I don't want to talk about Harper, R-a-y. You got that?"

Andy let go and Ray rubbed his neck and said, "I got it," and he walked away.

Andy looked down and saw an extension cord stretched between two palm trees pulled taut, something he wouldn't have done. Beyond the "trip wire" was a deep hole dug in the sand. Did Ray provoke him on purpose to lure him to trip and fall using a trap? Andy looked up and the camera operators and crew all looked down or away. Nobody wanted to look him in the eye. Andy needed to talk to Emma and see what she thought.

Down the beach Emma and Luann were "working" on a project with a tan, muscular crew member with a hard hat, no shirt, and six pack abs. He was showing the women how to use a nail gun. They were clearly enjoying themselves.

"Oh hi, hun," Emma said and asked, "How's the bar coming along?"

The muscular man reached out his hand and said, "I'm a big fan of your music."

"Are you local?" Andy asked.

"No, the producers flew me out. I'm Clay by the way."

Andy nodded, said thanks and asked Emma if he could have a word. The two took shelter under a palm tree for both shade and privacy. Little did either of them know the producers hid tiny cameras in the trees and all over the property. This covert, ambush filming wasn't in the contract—for good reason.

CHAPTER 19

Trudy Thomas and Tex Tillerson were sipping tropical drinks while sitting in oversized inner tubes floating down the lazy river pool that was a feature of the Hyatt hotel where they were staying.

"So, it's not as bad you imagined," Tex said while waving his drink around to highlight the lush scenery and setting of the hotel.

Despite being dressed in an oversized beach hat and a full-body swimsuit, Trudy was enjoying herself. "You were right, this isn't so bad."

"Isn't so bad? This is paradise and with your production plan I can see we are onto something special."

"Yeah, today when we did the cutaway confessionals with the sun setting in the background, the location was clearly the star."

"How are things going with some of the ideas we talked about to spice up the show?"

"I'm going to spring something on each cast member throughout the shoot. First up is Luann. I've got her bookie flying in this week. He's a real piece of work so this should be interesting."

"How much does Luann owe the guy?"

"$25,000, give or take."

"Wow!"

"I took care of it. I expensed $10,000, which he took in exchange for a chance to be on the show. He's going to offer Luann a winner-takes-all bet to wipe out her debt to him which I'll make sure she loses. We'll then have security haul him away. He's on board with it."

"You have a sick mind, you know that right?" Tex said, shaking his head. "How about a happy ending for a change?"

"I think the bloody tropics are turning you squidgy."

"Squidgy?"

"It's what we say back in Britain when someone gets soft and squishy, like you."

"And you're what we call, Texas Tough."

"I think you forget you're not from Texas, *Tex.*"

CHAPTER 20

Andy called another meeting of the gang of five at Kalapaki Joe's to talk about what the first week of filming revealed and to make sure they remained a united front.

"So I've got some good news and some bad news, which do you want first?" Andy asked.

"How about the good news," Lily said. "I've got some of my own to share, too."

Andy began, "Okay, with the amount of people working on the project we are making really good progress. Much faster than if we were weren't filming. It seems the artificial deadlines the producers set for the cast and crew to create added pressure is working. The beach bar is done except for the detail work and we already poured the foundation for all the other beachfront structures."

"What's the bad news, Boss," Ray wanted to know.

"I may be wrong about this but does anyone else get the sense the producers are trying to turn us against one another?" Andy asked.

The others looked around but nobody spoke, so Andy kept going. "You don't think it's odd they brought that Clay guy over and then split us up to have him work with just the two of you," Andy pointed at Emma and Luann.

"It's all in good fun," Emma said, dismissing Andy's suspicions.

Andy shook his head and said, "Lily, you said you had some good news to share?"

"Do you remember when I blessed the land when we first started?" Everyone nodded. "Well I didn't tell anyone this but I got a really bad feeling about the property and the inn when I did that."

Andy said, "And you're just telling us about this now?"

"Uh, yeah, but now that I'm working on the cultural center I can feel a shift in the spirit of the place. It's like the uhane are pleased with what we're trying to do."

"Uhane?" Andy asked.

"Ghosts," was Lily's reply.

CHAPTER 21

The producers pushed Andy and his crew to work on the beach-front projects first while Bradley and the local crew took on the bigger buildings in the middle of the property. The beach bungalows and staff areas would be built last. At least that's how Trudy hoped things would go. Andy agreed to work on the bar and grill, coffee and ice cream shop, and sports center first, but insisted the bungalows be built after that so they had a place to live. Andy was still living in his van, Emma was back at Poipu Shores, Ray's old bungalow was left standing for now, and Luann lived with Lily. Why the producers wanted the bar and grill done so soon quickly became clear.

Even though the kitchen wasn't ready yet, the bar was, and everyone—cast, crew, family and friends—made a beeline for it at the end of each day. However, the cameras never stopped rolling and that's the way Trudy and Tex intended it play out.

"Look at this place," Ray said as he walked through the tropical oasis and what could best be described as an outdoor version of Keoki's Paradise, the lush, island-style restaurant and bar Andy fell in love with months before.

Luann was quite proud and said so, "I know, we did it. Only this is just for us and the guests."

Andy corrected her, "We will also let the locals use it for free for community meetings and events. And, if someone walks up off the public beach they are welcome as well."

Lily smiled and nodded. Ray looked perplexed.

The open-air bar was covered with a thatched roof, but you could sit at the outdoor tables and with a cold drink in your hand, your feet in the warm sand, and enjoy a stunning view of the bay. It was perfection—and everyone helped make it happen under Andy's instruction and supervision.

Trudy and Tex walked up, completely overdressed and said, "What you guys built, it's beautiful. Stunning, really. Emma, why don't you go behind the counter and pull the tarp off the backbar? We have a surprise for you."

Emma walked over while the cameras rolled and the big reveal was... a fully stocked bar along with brand new glassware. Since everyone was currently drinking beer from an Igloo cooler, this was a big improvement.

"We have another surprise for you," Trudy announced. "We've brought in a guest bartender from Las Vegas to serve you drinks tonight."

Luann's knees went weak. A bartender from Vegas? Why Vegas? She was tempted to bolt but her curiosity got the better of her and she stayed put. When Trudy said, "Please welcome Carlos," Luann knew she was in trouble because from behind the building popped out her old bookie, Carlos Leon, better known by his nickname, "Ladykiller." The moniker wasn't because he was good with women, it was because it was rumored he'd murdered more than one over the years. Everyone cheered, except Luann who wondered what was happening.

"Hello Lu Lu," Carlos said with a Cheshire grin. "I see you

landed on your feet."

"Carlos," Luann spit out.

Sending the tension, everyone stopped cheering and wondered what was really going on. "This is my friend from the casino, he was also my bookie," Luann said, clearly embarrassed.

"You really were a lousy gambler, Lu Lu," Carlos said as he took his place behind the bar. Sure, he knew how to make drinks, but he was here to make trouble.

"Gather around everyone, I have a game I want to play."

"Not interested," Luann replied.

"What if I told you that if you win this next bet I will wipe out your debt to me?"

"All of it?"

"All of it."

"What if I lose?"

"Then I want everything you owe me, plus interest."

Emma walked around Carlos to the back of the bar and grabbed a bottle of high end tequila and said, "Shots for everyone!"

Andy rolled his eyes, but went along for the ride. As usual, it was three shots in a row, exactly what the producers intended—get Emma drunk and see what happens.

After the sun set and several more shots, an inebriated Luann said to Carlos as he mugged for the cameras while serving drinks, "You came all this way to collect from me Carlos, really?"

"Yup. One last bet, winner take all."

"When I win I want you to take off that stupid fedora and silk shirt and throw yourself in the ocean," Luann said, clearly fueled by liquid courage, she wasn't as afraid of Carlos the "Lady Killer" as she was back in her desert days.

Carlos gave her that creepy smile again and said, "If you lose, and you will, I want a…" Carlos caught himself, realizing he was on camera and said, "I will want to stick around. I like it here."

Lily stepped in and said, "What's the game?"

Emma poured herself a shot and slurred, "Yeah, C-a-r-l-o-s . What's the game?"

Carlos looked at Trudy and she nodded, so he said. "You ever heard of the *Newlywed Game*?"

"Yeah, but I'm single. You know that," Luann said.

"Your friends aren't."

Lily stepped in again, "You mean Andy and Emma?"

"Yup."

Lily looked over at Emma, she was smashed. "Alright, first thing tomorrow we meet here and play your stupid little game."

"No, we do it now. It will be fun."

Andy finally got involved. "Whatever she owes you, I'll pay it."

Carlos considered the offer but said, "It's not just about the money. Back home Lu Lu made me look like a fool when I couldn't find her and collect. I want to see her suffer, so I say we play now. Besides, if you and your wife know each other like you should, you have nothing to worry about."

Emma stumbled over and hung on her husband's arm. "We've got this, babe."

"Fine, let's play," Andy said. Not sure why he agreed, especially since this was being filmed.

Carlos clearly had help with his questions, and he had Andy and Emma answer them privately, separately, and somewhat honestly. To stage this bet-off to look like the actual game show, the producers had the crew act as the audience. Andy and Emma sat at opposite ends of a table, Luann was between them, and Carlos stood and acted as emcee. What could go wrong?

"Okay Lu Lu, I've asked each contestant the same three questions. If they get two out of three answers to match, all is forgiven. If two of their answers don't match, you owe me big time," Carlos said, really feeling comfortable in front of the camera now.

It only took a few minutes to ask each contestant the questions separately and get their replies.

"First question," Carlos said as the cameras zoomed in. "What was the first movie you saw together?"

Carlos checked his cards, one from Andy and the other from Emma so he already knew if they matched. "Emma, you said, *Ace Ventura*." Everyone clapped, not because they thought it was a good answer, but because they like the movie. "Andy, you said… *Dumb and Dummer*. So I guess you are a "Lawhooooooo-ser," Carlos said, mimicking the movie.

Andy and Emma looked at each other, saddened they didn't remember which movie they went to see together at the start of their relationship.

Luann stuck up for her friends and said, "Hey, both movies star Jim Carrey, so it would be real easy to mix them up."

Carlos laughed and said, "It seems with one question wrong these two will have to get the next two right, good luck with that Lu Lu."

"It's not over," Lu Lu said.

Now mimicking a line from the movie, *Dumb and Dumber*, Carlos said, "So you're telling me there's a chance."

"Just read the next question," Lu Lu said.

"Okay, the next question is, 'Is there a chance your partner ever strayed during your marriage?'"

Everyone quieted down and leaned in for the answer. "I'll spare you the drama, you both said no."

Andy and Emma smiled at each other, but both didn't seem as sure as their "no" answers implied.

"And now for the final question," Carlos paused, playing this to the hilt and wondering when this episode was going to air because he now had dreams of having his own reality show about a loan shark based in Las Vegas. He already had the title, "Lady Killer."

"Earth to Carlos," Luann said. "The last question, please."

"Right. Right. The third and final question is, 'What is the one wish you both share?'"

Even a narcissistic, sociopath like Carlos felt a twinge of pain when reading their answers, "You both said to have your son back."

Off camera Trudy and Tex subtly clinked their drinks together as the scene played out. Luann raised her fists in triumph. Carlos announced that drinks were on the house—which they were anyway.

Out of view Carlos forcibly pulled Luann aside. "I'm flying back to Vegas tomorrow and when I get back I'm telling everyone I tracked you all the way to Hawaii and made you pay."

"Okay," Luann said, not wanting to provoke Carlos since she got what she wanted.

"Are you feelin' me?" Carlos asked.

"I'm feelin' you. You came all this way to make me pay."

"Exactly. I don't expect to see you again so this is good-bye... for good."

Later that night when the cameras were turned off and everyone went home, Andy and Emma sat alone in the sand staring out at the moonlit bay.

"Do you think he's out there?" Emma asked, a bottle of tequila by her side.

"I'd like to think so, but I know he's not. If he were I would go to him. I would swim out there and not stop until I found him."

"Or die?"

"If it meant I could be with Harper, yes."

Emma handed Andy the bottle and said, "It helps, a little."

Andy took a swig and said. "I have everything I ever wanted, fame, fortune, and a project I can call my own. No matter what I do or have, nothing fills the hole inside of me and sadness lurks around every corner. I'm broken."

"I know how you feel, I do."

Andy turned and looked at Emma but didn't say anything. After Harper's death he couldn't look at Emma, or even be in the same room—the one person who understood he was drowning, and he pushed her away. He had to. When he saw her it triggered emotions like anger, shame, and guilt.

"What? What are you thinking?" Emma asked.

"In that stupid game when that joker, what's his name?"

"Carlos."

"When Carlos asked if you'd been faithful, was your answer honest? Have you been?"

"Andy, there's something you should know…"

CHAPTER 22

Andy understood the valuable exposure the show, *Made Inn Hawaii* would provide, but the bright lights and cameras were a lesser priority for him than it was to the others. His goal was to put his heart and soul into building this big beautiful inn and then sharing it with others. Andy was eager to dig in and do the more demanding part of the plans. The producers had him working on small projects he could quickly complete, which was apparently better for filming. Andy was more than happy to get out of the limelight and hand off the smaller stuff off to others so he could work on the larger structures. Plus he wanted to put some distance between himself and Emma.

Andy bought his buddy Bradley a matching Mercedes Sprinter van and parked it just a few feet away from his. This allowed them to live onsite, and check in with each other first thing in the morning, or after everyone left for the day.

Each van came with a kitchenette so the two took turns making coffee and breakfast and sitting at the pseudo bistro-like setup the two built out of scrap wood. These early morning meetings allowed the old friends to speak freely about the cast and crew.

"Andy, did you see this?" Bradley pointed to a picture in

the well-worn, dog-eared pages of the accessories catalog for the Sprinters, now spread open on the table.

"You want to order a safe that bolts onto the back bumper?"

"It's not a safe, it's a locking storage locker. There's a few things I want to make sure I keep away from prying eyes."

Andy nodded, knowing exactly what Bradley meant. "How much is it?"

"With shipping, about a grand."

"I'll order two of them."

"Thanks, buddy."

"Hey, I owe you big time for dropping everything to come out here and help."

"That's funny. I was thinking I should be thanking you for allowing me to be here. I love this place and I love this project." It wasn't like Bradley lived large on the mainland. Like Andy, he lost everything to storms in Slidell and was so busy helping others rebuild he never got around to putting his own house in order.

"Thanks to you, things here are really coming together—despite the distraction of the show."

"We have some hardworking and talented people on this crew, and we've got a lot of them. It's the first time I've had more than enough help on site. That said, we're getting to the point where we're gonna need more tradesmen. As you know the cement, plumbing, and electrical contractors are all awesome. We've got roofing, painting, and HVAC specialists lined up, but besides the two of us, we don't have enough finishing people to do all the windows, doors, and interior stuff. Not to mention we need help with the drywall and tile, too."

"I like that we're keeping it local and that we're paying top dollar."

"I agree. Speaking of hiring tradespeople, I know you tasked Luann, Lily, and Emma to handle the interior design, but in my experience we should be further along with that by now. I think it's great they're pitching in on your pet projects, but…"

"Whoa. Whoa. Whoa. The bar, sports center, and outdoor areas aren't just pet projects, they're critically important," Andy insisted.

"Whatever you gotta tell yourself to get through the day."

"Underneath that tough guy exterior is a real funny guy."

"Yeah, right. What I'm getting at is they could use some help. A local interior designer stopped by and gave me her card. I think you should meet with her."

"Why don't you do it?" Andy asked.

"It's not my job and besides, your wife would kill me for stepping on her toes, and Luann and Lily would probably hate every design choice I made."

"True dat."

"Think of it as you doing Emma a favor. Here's her card."

Staring at the card Andy exclaimed, "She's in Princeville. That's on the other side of the island."

"So it is."

With coffee in hand Andy and Bradley walked the entirety of the site, and since it was a Sunday, nobody was around to bother them as they made notes and talked things through. The inn and surrounding structures were starting to take shape, but they were a long way off from being completed.

They finished the tour at the far corner of the property where the bungalows were to be built. "When will the supplies to start on these arrive?" Andy asked.

"Most of them are here. We can start on them after we finish framing the other dozen or so structures."

"So you mean next month."

"No, I mean in a couple of weeks, unless *you* want to do it."

"Yeah, well I was on tour when you were getting your Hawaii general contractor's license, so I probably shouldn't push the envelope, but I can help."

"The two general contractors that came with the architect are really the ones to talk to. As you know they've been on top of everything."

"I hardly ever talk to them anymore now that I'm part of the show."

"They're good people. I know you think it's me that's keeping this train on the tracks, but those two run the smoothest and cleanest job sites I've ever been a part of. And, like me they want no part of being on the show, so it's working out perfectly."

Ray ran over, excited and out of breath. "Remember when you said we could get a small boat for taking guests out snorkeling?"

"Vaguely."

"I found a super good, Ka'amiana deal on a 15-foot Zodiac with a 50 horsepower engine, and a trailer. It holds six people and only drafts a few inches so it would be perfect for the shallows out front."

"How much?"

"$15,000, which is half what it *should* cost."

"Is it stolen?" Bradley asked.

"Define stolen," Ray said with a straight face. Then added, "Of course it's not stolen. It's almost brand new, but got slightly damaged during the storm, but it's mostly cosmetic stuff which I can easily fix."

"Do you have a picture of it."

"Better. I towed it here for a test run. It's over by the sports center, where we can launch it."

Andy and Bradley looked at each other and shrugged.

CHAPTER 23

Bradley left to do some shopping in town, so Andy followed Ray to where the Zodiac was sitting on a trailer behind the beater truck Ray drove before getting his new and larger company truck.

"So, what do you think?"

"Man, this is like new, new." Andy marveled as he walked up to the boat.

"I know, the damage is all over here," and Ray showed him a few small things that would need a little work on the other side. "It's all gassed up and ready to go. Want to take it out?"

"Yeah, let's do it. Let me grab some beers from the bar."

"Already got 'em boss, and a couple of masks so we can check out the outer reef."

"Hot damn," Andy said, and hopped in. "Ever launch a boat like this, Ray?"

"Not exactly, but you know I'm a fast learner."

Andy showed him what to do and Ray backed the trailer over the plywood planks Andy put down to keep the truck from getting stuck in the sand. In just a foot of water the white rubber boat with a hard bottom glided out into one of the few places in the shallows with a sandy bottom.

Andy went to the center console and lowered the engine as he'd done many times before back home, turned the key and the little Honda outboard came to life.

Ray ran down the beach after parking his truck and sort of hopped up and rolled into the boat. "Isn't this great?"

"I have to admit, this feels good. Real good," Andy said as he slowly backed up and spun the boat around. "Ray, you know this bay as well as anyone. You're gonna need to tell me where all the cuts in the reef are. We'll take it slow."

Ray knew the reef like the back of his hand and he guided Andy through it as they zig zagged their way their way to the barrier reef and skirted along it until they came to the opening that led to deeper water.

"I've got fifteen feet on the depth finder and no wind, let's open 'er up and see what she can do," Andy said as they raced along the coast at a comfortable 25 mph. He looked to his left and took in the view from the water of what was becoming a beautiful inn designed and built to help people deal with loss—and that's when it hit him. The last time he was out here was when he was looking for Harper, long after the search parties had given up.

"Why are we slowing down?" Ray asked.

As Andy brought the boat to an idle he replied, "Why don't you take the wheel while I drink one of those beers you brought."

"Yeah, sure. So what do you think about the boat?" Ray asked as he handed Andy a beer.

"I love it, it's perfect. Let's buy it"

"Awesome. Well hang onto your hat because we're heading for Kipu Kai beach."

Andy knew all about Kipu Kai. It was only two bays away, but there was a night and day difference from "his" bay where the inn was situated and this one. He looked into buying the property, but because the beach is so beautiful, the owners weren't selling and it was out of his price range anyway. Andy now knew it would eventually be a part of the stretch of land and beach that Emma sold to the state to create a preserve. It was a case of life imitating art because Kipu Kai was featured in the film *Descendants* starring George Clooney, a film about the value of the land, and his love for his wife.

As soon as they rounded the bend the blue water, empty stretch of beach, and the cove in the corner were as picturesque as he remembered them.

"You can't get here by car you know," Ray told Andy as he powered down.

"I know. You have to hike in," Andy said.

"Or boat in," Ray boasted and slapped Andy on arm.

"Right. I mean look at this place, it's perfect. The water, it's so blue. Can you imagine if we had this kind of big sandy beach?"

"I'm glad they gonna keep it like this," Ray said.

"Yeah, me too. Slow down and look out for turtles, they're everywhere."

"Let's beach it over there in the corner cove, I want to go for a swim," Ray said, and Andy agreed.

Other than a boat or two that passed by, Ray and Andy were all alone in this pristine paradise. The sun was hot, the beers were cold, and the water was crystal clear. The two enjoyed a lazy Sunday hanging out at the best kept secret on the island.

Sitting in the sand, Ray said, "The guests would love it here."

"You're probably right, but I don't want to be the one to ruin it by taking tourists here. I say we keep today between us."

"You know what, boss. You're an alright guy... for a haole," Ray joked.

"Mahalo," Was all Andy said, not sure if it was an insult or a compliment.

At the end of a long day the two sunburned boaters returned to Harper's Bay, as Andy liked to call it, with just enough time left to get a snorkel session in along the barrier reef.

"Ray you coming?" Andy said as he finished his beer and slipped backward over the rounded edge of the boat and into the water as a diver would do.

"I'm right behind you, I'll set the anchor," Ray announced.

The snorkeling was incredible and Andy lost track of time. He'd bump into Ray here and there as they both explored all aspects of the reef and followed the incredible array of tropical fish around. It was Andy who noticed it was getting dark. Looking around he saw Ray just a few feet away.

"Ray, we gotta go," Andy said and pointed to his Rolex Submariner watch. After drinking that last beer he felt lightheaded and woozy but he pushed on. It was probably a combination of heatstroke and dehydration making his arms and legs feel weighted down. He was done for the day.

"Sounds good," Ray called back.

Andy looked around and said, "Hey Ray, where's the boat?"

Andy slowly swam over to where Ray was and they both looked around, stunned the boat was gone.

"You anchored the boat, right?" Andy asked.

"Yeah, right over there in the sandy bottom."

The two swam over to the spot and right away it was obvious what happened. The anchor was there, along with the chain and rope... lying on the bottom.

Andy titled his mask back on his head and sure enough, the Zodiac was visible in the distance, slowly drifting toward shore and the inn. The problem was it was a long, treacherous swim to the beach in the best of circumstances, but right now the tide was bottoming out and it was quickly getting dark, two things that worked against them.

The good news was Ray knew his way around the reef. The bad news was for Ray to find his way back to the beach required light and a circuitous route that would take forever. Also, only Bradley knew they were out on the water so it was unlikely any help was on the way.

"I can swim to the boat and come back and get you," Ray said, not sure what to do.

Andy didn't answer because he couldn't—he was suddenly overcome with tightness and pain in his chest as he struggled to breathe while feeling disoriented and confused. Andy was treading water, but fading fast.

"I'm going to get help, hang in there," Ray said, and he was gone.

CHAPTER 24

Emma and Luann were making the most of their Sunday off by driving to Polihale State Beach on the west side of the island. A girls' trip and a day away from the hard work on the inn and bright lights of the cameras.

Luann was the designated driver since it was a given that Emma would start the day with a cocktail or two at breakfast and keep it going through the afternoon and into the evening. Besides, they were making the trip in Luann's new Jeep. Now that she didn't owe Carlos any money and was living rent free she saved her paychecks and purchased a used Jeep on the cheap from a rental car company. She then went about making it look more local by bedazzling it with floral print seat covers, surf shop stickers, and a kukui nut necklace strung from the rearview mirror. It was a tangible sign she was turning her life around.

The two detoured through the tourist town of Hanapepe to look at local art, stopped for bagels and coffee at Grinds, and went to the Big Save in Waimea to stock up for the rough ride and long day at the deserted beach at the end of the road.

"Does the stereo work?" Emma yelled as they sped along. With the top off it was hard to hear.

"Only the radio. Just turn it on, it's already set to Island 98.9. Hawaiian hits."

"Perfect," Emma said and turned it on and up.

On the way they first passed the historic Plantation Inn and Emma insisted they stop to visit this secluded property that was a lot like theirs.

Then, further down the road it was a quick stop at The Pacific Missile Range Facility, better known as Barking Sands. Somewhere Emma had heard that Shenanigans, the bar on base was worth checking out—only to discover it was closed on Sundays.

Now it was a straight shot to the beach and thanks to the Jeep, they confidently traversed the bumpy dirt road to Polihale, which seemed to go on forever, until they reached the point where almost everyone turns right—they went left and were able to find their own improvised parking spot and easy access to the beach. When they climbed the sand dune and looked out they took in the most beautiful and extensive stretch of sand and sea in the world, and there was nobody else in sight. Paradise.

"Can you believe this?" Emma exclaimed running across the warm white sand like a kid.

Luann followed, slowed by the cooler and beach chair she was lugging along.

Emma came back to help, but couldn't contain her enthusiasm. "This is amazing!"

It took two trips from the Jeep to the beach, but now they were set for the day. They had matching beach chairs and umbrellas, a cooler full of drinks and snacks—mostly drinks—and a portable speaker. But the best thing they brought was the last thing they bought—inflatable inner tubes. The ocean looked like a lake, with no waves to speak of and just a touch of wind. The two tied their inner tubes together and floated side by side in the ocean with drinks in hand. It was as good as it gets.

"Luann, this is my new happy place. I'm so glad we did this."

"I know. I'm calling this my mental health day. Things have been so crazy lately. I love living with my auntie, but I just needed a day away," Luann admitted.

"So what's was the deal with you and Carlos," Emma asked. "Was he *just* your bookie?"

"Carlos? Yeah, trust me, he was *just* my bookie."

"I thought maybe I sensed something more."

"Emma, have you not figured it out yet?"

"Figured what out?"

"I'm not into guys."

"Oh."

"Surprise!"

"I had no idea."

"It's not like I keep it a secret. It's just that I don't advertise it."

"Is there someone you have your eye on?"

"You mean, besides you."

"Me?"

"I'm kidding. Although you would be quite a catch. There's a mainlander on the crew, I think her name is Christy. I haven't gotten up the nerve to talk to her yet, but I will. Now let me ask you something. The other night when Carlos asked you and Andy if you cheated, did you tell truth?"

"Yes, and no."

"What does that mean?"

"Technically, I was never *with* anyone, but in a way what I did was worse."

"What do you mean?"

"I became emotionally involved with one of my male co-workers."

"Does Andy know?"

"He does now. I told him just the other night."

"How did he take it?"

"Not well. He was hurt and felt betrayed. I totally understand. I get it. He sees Jim and Lizzy…"

"Jim and Lizzy McDaniel?"

"Yeah, he sees their relationship and he wants that for us, but I just don't know."

"Are you two *not* together right now?"

"I'm not sure. I'm just not sure."

CHAPTER 25

Out of the corner of his eye while he thrashed about Andy saw Ray swim away as dusk put a blanket over the last of the light left from the setting sun. The pain in his chest was still great and it was compounded by the cramping in his legs and the fatigue throughout his body. Although the water was warm, he was shivering as if it were ice cold. His rapid breathing made him feel dizzy and the darkness gave him cause for concern, but after a minute or two of pure panic he was able to pull himself together.

Andy knew he was in trouble, and that maybe this was his time. He also knew his chances of surviving a heart attack in the open ocean at night were slim, so he let go of his fear and embraced death.

Andy pulled his mask off and rolled onto his back so he could look up at the night sky. It was beautiful. Why he didn't do this before, he wasn't sure. He let the pain wash over him and he just floated, which had a calming effect. His breathing normalized, his cramps went away, and the pain in his chest and left side were now manageable. Andy wondered if this is what it was like for Harper in his last minutes of life. Did he fight to live until the end or did he eventually let go when he was pulled out to sea to drown on his own terms? Andy closed his eyes to remember that day.

It was the second to last day of their first trip to Kauai four years earlier, a place all three wanted to go and Andy and Emma used Harper's first spring break as a high school freshman as an excuse. Back then they couldn't afford much so they booked a bargain hotel with no beach access in Lihue. Harper loved the ocean so they spent each day exploring different beaches on both sides of the island.

This day it was going to be paddle boarding in Nawiliwili Bay, lunch at Dukes, and then they would head over to Shipwreck Beach, a medium-size stretch of sand squeezed in between the Hyatt and where the inn sits. One of the attractions—other than the wave that breaks out front—is the cliff that juts out from the point. Harrison Ford and Anne Hecht made the 40-foot jump in the film, *Six Days, Seven Nights*. It's plenty deep if you jump out far enough, but around the rocks it's shallow and there can be big waves crashing against them along with strong and swift currents that can quickly pull a person out to sea—and has. Several people have lost their lives there.

The trio didn't get to Shipwreck's until late in the afternoon. They lucked into a parking spot by the showers and found there was plenty of room on the sand. Right away Harper wanted to jump off the cliff, but Emma said no, even though there were local teenagers jumping off despite the pounding surf below. Andy agreed with Emma. It looked dangerous. Instead, they left their towels and the three walked the short distance to crash the Hyatt's salt water lagoon. It was the perfect peaceful place to snorkel, kayak, or just float around in the calm waters. Andy and Emma grabbed tropical drinks from the bar while Harper snorkeled. It was the best day, until it wasn't.

Unbeknownst to Andy and Emma, their teenage son snorkeled to a far corner of the lagoon and snuck off back to the beach to jump off the cliff. This is when the nightmare began. After thirty minutes the Clarkes noticed Harper was nowhere to be seen, but they figured he was still exploring the lagoon. After an hour the couple began to worry and they both swam out into the lagoon to search for their son, more mad he hadn't at least checked in than concerned for his safety in the four-foot deep man-made inlet. With no sight of their son, the two started to panic and packed up to head back to their rental car. Maybe Harper was bored and wanted to leave so he showered off and was waiting for them in the parking lot. They would give their son a piece of their mind and that would be that.

When they got to the rental car they sensed something was wrong. A woman ran by with her phone to her ear. Others were swimming out to the point. Andy dropped what he was holding and made a mad dash for the water. Somehow he knew. He just knew.

A crowd formed at the waters edge as close to the cliff as safely possible—the shore break was intense and dangerous with the rocks just to the left. Emma heard someone say a teenager jumped off and then disappeared. Her heart sunk. Could it be Harper? No. No way.

Andy fought the waves and the currents and made it to the spot directly under the overhang. The water was churned up by the stormy seas so he couldn't see anything, but he dove down anyway. Nothing. He repeated this several times until someone wrapped an arm around him and pulled him up from behind. When they surfaced the lifeguard tried to pull him to the rescue boat, but Andy fought him off and broke free.

"It's my boy! It's my son!" Andy yelled as he swam off.

The lifeguard swam after him and yelled, "We got this. Help is on the way."

As if on cue, lifeguards on jet skis raced by and Andy could hear a helicopter overhead. Exhausted, he followed the lifeguard back to the boat—one of two now on scene. Once on board, Andy was shaking from adrenaline and fear.

"What happened?" Andy asked.

"One the locals reported that a tourist kid took a running start to make sure he cleared the rocky shallow area but he tripped at the last second and tumbled in. The fall messed up his timing and instead of landing on top of an incoming wave, he landed while the water was being sucked back out to sea."

Andy held his face in his hands as he listened. This couldn't be happening. Maybe Harper was in the crowd and he missed him. Maybe it was someone else's son, a thought he fought off because as bad as that sounded, he also wished it was true.

"What color trunks was your son wearing?" The lifeguard asked.

"Uh, he um, he had on black trunks. Why?"

"That fits with the description we got of the jumper."

"Doesn't almost everyone wear black trunks?" Andy asked.

"Yeah, it's a Hawaiian thing. Let's hold out hope your son is safe on the beach, yeah?"

Andy nodded.

"My name is Makua, which also means parent in Hawaiian. We gonna do everything we can to find your boy. I have a son, too, so I understand how you feel. Just sit tight, we got this."

Andy thought about it for a few seconds and then flung off the blanket he'd been given and jumped back in the water. If it *was* Harper out there, he wasn't going to sit by and watch, he was going to save his son—or die trying.

The lifeguards and Coast Guard searched until well past dark, but suspended the search until first light. The Hyatt offered the grieving parents a complimentary room, but instead Andy spent the night on the beach hoping to hear his son's voice cry out for help so he could swim in and save him. He also frantically ran up and down the Mahaulepu trail which was high ground and parallel to the beach. Eventually exhaustion got him and he passed out on the trail.

When Andy awoke at dawn he was covered in dirt, dried sweat, and blood. Now that the adrenaline rush had worn off, he ached all over. As the sun came up he noticed something else, strange bruises on his torso. Andy later learned the entire area—including the inn—were known to be prone to paranormal activity. He didn't care because however he got the bruises it woke him up so he could resume his solo search and rescue attempt. In the distance Andy heard a helicopter and jet skis approaching. He still had hope that Harper survived the night.

After two full days the search was called off and Harper was presumed deceased. Emma was understandably inconsolable. She couldn't accept that Harper was gone and the guilt she felt believing she could have prevented his death consumed her. She was taken to the old hospital in Kapaa for observation.

For the first week of a two-week stay, Andy visited Emma in the morning and then spent the rest of his day walking the trail and searching the beaches and bays along the coast east and west of the cliff looking for his lost son's body. His grief and guilt were overwhelming, but he pressed on. It was on one of these long treks along the shoreline Andy discovered the deserted inn and its beachfront property. He began formulating a plan to make this his home base where he would wait for Harper to return. He realized how crazy that sounded, but with all the "what if" scenarios that ran through his head (maybe Andy was rescued by a passing boat but had amnesia) he wanted to be close by, just in case.

Eventually, the grief-stricken couple returned to Slidell, Louisiana. Emotionally, they were a mess. Financially, it was even worse. The hurricane wiped out their home just before it was foreclosed on. It was a blessing in disguise. The insurance money bailed them out. Rebuilding the town became Andy's mission (and a way to earn a living) and at night he played music around town—both kept his mind busy. Moving to Baton Rouge and throwing herself into her work suited Emma as well.

Then the hit song, and the money that came with it, changed everything.

CHAPTER 26

Bradley was using the newly installed BBQ on the beach to cook up some dinner. It was the maiden voyage for the state-of-the-art grill and he felt it should be tested, and he was just the person to do it. Bradley was planning to surprise Andy with a steak dinner when he returned from his day of boating.

Fiddling with the controls of the oversized grill and focusing on keeping an eye on the thick pieces of meat he paid a small fortune for and was hoping to get just right was when he saw Ray out of the corner of his eye. If he didn't know better he would have said Ray was running along the bushes to stay out of sight. He assumed Andy would follow in a few minutes so he turned the burners up just a little.

When the steaks were ready and Andy was nowhere to be seen, Bradley turned the heat down and walked to where the boat was launched earlier that day.

Floating free just off the beach was the Zodiac. Bradley thought that was odd, especially combined with Ray's strange behavior. Bradley waded in, careful to avoid the reef to grab the bowline and pull the boat in. Once the boat was pulled up on the sand, Bradley climbed in and checked to see if the key was in the ignition. It was. Then he checked the gauges to make sure there was plenty of fuel. There was. So where was Andy? His stuff was still on board, but there was no sign of his friend.

Bradley pushed the boat back in the water but left the engine raised. Instead he used the oar as a pole to push the boat out to slightly deeper water. He lowered the motor a little, but kept it trimmed up before turning the key. Very slowly and carefully Bradley made his way to the outer reef and used the search light to navigate the shallows. The incoming tide helped, but it was still touch and go until he reached the small channel that led to the open ocean. That's when he spotted something. He shined the light in that direction and at first it looked like a sleeping manatee, but he knew they didn't live here in the islands. When he reached the object he quickly realized it was Andy, floating facedown in the ocean, and just in time.

CHAPTER 27

"You know you're like a cat, right?" Doctor Tanaka stated as he checked in on Andy.

"Because I have nine lives Doc?" Andy answered with a grin.

"By my count, you only have a couple left."

"If that," Andy agreed.

"You dodged another bullet this time, so to speak," Doctor Tanaka stated. "Although knowing you, a gun shot wound is still a possibility."

It was true. Other than being shot at, he'd experienced almost every other way to die imaginable—and yet he'd survived. Was someone looking out for him while someone else was looking to harm him?

Andy was extremely lucky and unlucky at the same time. The doctors diagnosed him as having a panic attack and not a heart attack. Other than that he just had some cuts and bruises and mild hypothermia, but the doctor wouldn't release him until he had a complete psych exam—that was the unlucky part... Andy wasn't 100% sure he'd pass.

"There's someone here to see you," Dr. Tanaka said on his way out of Andy's hospital room.

Bradley knocked and entered the room. "He's alive."

"Thanks to you."

"Yeah, well a blind squirrel and all that. I'm just glad I found you when I did."

"Me, too."

"So, I've got some news for you, and you're not gonna like it," Bradley said and pulled the only chair in the room close to the head of the bed so the two friends could speak in confidence.

"Why the secrecy?"

"Did you know the entire work site was rigged with cameras and microphones? They were all over the place, and it was Ray who installed them for the producers."

"Ray?"

"Yeah, Ray. It turns out they paid him extra to plant the surveillance equipment."

"No, not Ray?"

"He knew where on property to avoid if he didn't want to be seen or heard, but if I were you, I'd ask to review that footage, maybe he made a mistake."

"I will."

"There's more. After I got you to shore and the ambulance came, I went looking for him. Before I got the boat I saw Ray run by while you were out there drowning."

"Maybe he was going to get help."

"Not a chance. He went straight to Emma's condo to tell her you were dead and to profess his love for her."

"What the…?"

"He left you for dead, Andy, and there's more. He's the one who's been trying to kill you."

"How do you know?"

"He told me."

"He just told you?"

Bradley raised an eyebrow and said, "I made him *want* to tell me. I can be pretty persuasive when I want to be and I had the help of a few items I stored in my lockbox. If I go to jail for what I did, so be it—at least I'll be in Hawaii"

"Is he dead?" Andy whispered.

"If we were back home in the Bayou he would be. I would have bled him dry for information and then fed him to the gators."

"So where is he now?"

"I don't know, I let him go, sort of."

"Okay, I don't need to know. What else did he say?"

"You didn't fall off the roof by accident. He sprayed the area near the ladder with silicone. You also didn't bang your head on a beam, he struck you with a board."

"Let me guess, he tampered with the breaker box so I would get electrocuted."

"Yup. He also tried other times to take you out, but failed."

Andy shook his head, "Man, I read him all wrong."

"Apparently he wanted your wife and the inn and had no problem with killing you and making it look like an accident to make his delusional dream come true."

"I taught him about the trade, bought him anything and everything he asked for—and more. I thought we were friends."

"More like Frenemies."

"So he thought with me out of the way he would just slide in and take over my life? Did Emma know about his plan? Was she in on it?"

"I don't think so, but that's something you two will have to talk about. Has she been by to see you yet?"

"No… she hasn't," Andy said slowly.

"Interesting," Bradley said, again with that raised eyebrow look.

CHAPTER 28

Luann, Emma, and Lily sat in silence waiting to see the interior designer. The producers wanted to send a camera crew along knowing there could be some conversations that would make for good television. The three declined and instead did confessionals in front of the camera about Ray—closeup cutaways the producers could edit in later. Emma also sat for a long one-on-one interview about Andy, but this was the first time the three women were all together since Andy was found barely alive.

"How are you holding up, Emma?" Luann asked.

"I'm angry, shocked, ashamed, and relieved all at the same time. All I can think of is how did I miss it?"

"We all did, Emma. All of us misread Ray," Luann said.

"I knew," Lily whispered.

"What do you mean you knew?" Emma asked Lily.

"I didn't *know*, I just suspected there was something off with Ray," Lily said. "While you were all off island I would stop by to see him and he started to open up to me, you know, little things—little things that didn't add up and looking back now were red flags. I'm sorry I didn't say anything, but it was Ray, you know."

"It's okay, Lily," Emma said.

"What now?" Luann asked.

"I think I now have a real reason you can talk to Christy to see what she knows," Emma said with a wink to Luann.

"Is there something *I* should know?" Lily asked them both.

"It's nothing auntie," Luann replied.

The three met with the interior designer for hours, but Emma left after the big decisions were made to go see her husband in the hospital. Something she knew she should have done right away, not after a long delay. She would tell Andy she knew he was fine and that it was important to take care of the design details of the inn. Only that wasn't the truth.

She knew she hurt him deeply when she admitted to having an emotional affair with someone she'd worked with. She also wondered if she sent mixed signals to Ray that were misread and led to his attempts to try and harm her husband. Maybe the biggest realization of all was admitting she would never be able to look at Andy and not think about Harper and want to run away.

The day Harper disappeared, Andy's reaction was to try and rescue their son—almost dying doing it. Her reaction was to retreat into herself and eventually recede into drugs and alcohol.

This project to build something so close to where Harper went missing was both a blessing and a curse. It felt good to be doing something to help others with their grief, but if she was being honest, she was still in a great deal of pain and the constant reminders of Harper were not helping. Parents aren't supposed to outlive their kids and they aren't built to cope with that kind of pain—at least she wasn't.

Andy was dealing with Harper's death differently. He was

channeling his pain into his songs and his plans for the inn—and was succeeding on both counts. Her pain was like a ringing in her ears, it was always there. Always. Nothing she did made it go away. Nothing filled the void in her life that losing her only son left.

What made it worse was the fact there was no closure. His body being found might have helped. For Andy, the fact Harper was just "out there" gave him a glimmer of hope. For her, being able to bury her son was the clear ending she needed to allow for a healthier beginning on her journey with grief. That longing for an end to the pain meant nothing made her happy. Nothing had any meaning.

Andy's grief was different. His pain seemed to come and go like waves on the beach. Occasionally a rogue wave would come crashing in and hold him down, but he always surfaced and kept going, swimming toward the horizon with hope in his heart.

It was now crystal clear what she should do. Emma would go to the hospital and tell Andy she was heading home, back to the mainland, but would come back when the inn was finished and say goodbye for good to Andy, Kauai, and most of all, to Harper. It suddenly felt like she knew how to move forward.

CHAPTER 29

When Andy returned to the job site he was impressed with the tremendous progress the crew made in his short absence. With the workday done, Andy was expecting to meet with his team and discuss the details of the design and the construction schedule to see where he was needed next.

Instead, Bradley drove him straight to the beach bar where everyone was gathered and maybe just a *little bit* lathered up. As soon as he stepped out of the truck everyone cheered. Of course the film crew caught the scene from every angle. "The Hero Returns," would likely be the title of the series segment.

Bradley stood on a table facing the group that gathered around Andy and said, "Without this man, none of this would be possible." Everyone cheered—Andy, too. Only Bradley wasn't talking about Andy, he was referring to someone else. From around the corner Jim McDaniel appeared and everyone went wild. Andy was so happy to see his friend again and the two had a big ole man hug.

Bradley continued, "Jim McDaniel everyone. Jim is here to support Andy who is going to play us some of his own songs."

Andy looked over at Bradley, not mad at all, but grateful for a real friend who could make something like this happen.

Jim McDaniel stood up on the table next to Bradley and said, "It was music that first brought Andy and I together, but while we were on the road for weeks at a time, it became clear we were brothers from another mother. My wife says we're two peas in a pod. It's probably 'cause we're both from Louisiana and live and die with each Saints game, love us some spicy cajun cookin', and of course, have to start our day with a beignet from Cafe du Monde. Ain't that right, Andy?"

"True dat," was his reply.

"So instead of taking you to New Orleans, Andy, I brought New Orleans to you," Jim said with a big grin. "First, I flew in a couple of chefs from back home who specialize in creole cooking. They're in the kitchen right now making enough jambalaya to go around. I also had them bring a big batch of beignets for dessert."

Bradley was clearly loving this, and so were the producers who were given a heads up ahead of time so it was only a surprise to some that there was one more big reveal. "Is that all you brought with you?" Bradley yelled out. "What about our love of the Saints? You got anything for that?"

As planned, the two hammed it up and then Jim said, "Well, I didn't have to go to New Orleans for this surprise since Drew Brees lives right here on Kauai. Drew, come on out." And with that the Saints Super Bowl quarterback and part-time North shore resident walked out to even louder cheering.

The loudest cheer of all came when Jim McDaniel announced the drinks were on the house and to get ready for the show starting soon.

The producers and Jim McDaniel's people brought in a small stage, sound system, some modest lighting, and set it up with the ocean as the backdrop. Andy took the stage alone with Jim seated in the front row. The extra mic, stool, and guitar was a clue the megastar would be joining in at some point, but for now the show was all Andy's and when he walked onstage, he owned it. He was coming into his own as performer.

"Before I begin, I have a few things I want to say. To everyone here who has helped make my dream come true by building this special place from the ground up, I want you to know I appreciate you more than you'll ever know. All I ever wanted to do was wear a tool belt and build things, and you guys get to do that everyday. In some ways I envy you. Hey, maybe we'll market an aftershave that smells like sawdust for those of us who truly love what we do." Everyone laughed.

"I also want to thank all the super smart people who knew how to get this thing done—the architects, general contractors, and of course, my wife. Thank you to all the local contractors on the crew who did everything the right way so we could pass every inspection with flying colors.

"You probably heard I almost died… again. The truth is, if it wasn't for Bradley, I wouldn't be here right now.

"Lily and Luann, I can't thank you enough for putting your heart and soul into this project.

"Last, but certainly not least, to Jim McDaniel, I love you, man. This guy is a big star with a big heart. I will never, ever be able to repay you for what you've done for me, but what I know about you is you would never expect me to."

As Andy always did when on tour, he looked up to the sky and said a quick prayer for his son before he sang the first song of the set. This time Andy added these words and said them right into the camera just a few feet from his face, "Sometimes we must break apart completely in order to rebuild better." For the producers watching, this was ratings gold.

To say it was a night to remember would be the biggest understatement of all time. Nobody would ever forget Andy's heartfelt performance, or the sing-alongs with Jim McDaniel, or the food. Maybe the best part was the two played a couple of extended versions of cajun-blues tunes that were New Orleans classics and had *everyone* up and dancing in the sand. It was a sight to see. The producers would make sure nobody forgot the fun by capturing it all for the viewing audience.

After almost everyone left—including the celebrities, chefs, and Emma—Andy and just a few of the crew sat around the fire pit on the warm tropical night. Luann was cozied up to Christy. Bradley never left his friend's side with Ray still unaccounted for. Seated across from them was someone Andy didn't recognize, so he went over and sat next to her.

"Hi, I'm Andy Clarke. I don't recall seeing you before. Are you with the show?"

"Oh God no. I'm an interior designer."

"Really. Are you the one who sent your sketches to my hospital room?"

"Guilty. I heard about this project and what it would mean to so many people and I just had to be involved. So yeah, I had my sister who is a nurse put them in your room."

"Hmmmmmmm."

"I hope you're not mad. I also went through the proper channels and met with your wife and staff as well."

"Are you kidding? Anyone that passionate about what they do is someone I want to work with."

"So you liked my drawings and the samples I left?"

"They're not at all what I envisioned," Andy said matter of factly and paused for effect, "They're better than I could have ever hoped for. I love them."

"Oh, what a relief. You really got me there."

"You are super talented..." Andy stopped because he didn't know her name.

"Amanda. Amanda Bennett."

"Where are you from Amanda?"

"Well, if you must know, I went to Tulane."

"Is the whole state of Louisiana on Kauai right now or what?"

They both laughed and Amanda blushed. Bradley watched the whole thing unfold and noticed the chemistry between the two, not sure what to do about it—if anything.

CHAPTER 30

Before Emma headed back to Louisiana she agreed to come by the worksite for some final on-camera confessionals and pose for promotional pictures with Andy. She hoped the camera couldn't tell her smile was fake. Her loving and happy relationship with Andy—fake. Her excitement about the inn being completed wasn't faked, but Emma was looking forward to moving on with her life. She couldn't help thinking as the cameras clicked away was, "Elvis has left the building."

Andy, being a little more experienced at publicity shots, was more convincing in his role as happy husband and proud developer. The only thing he had to fake was the part about working with Emma. The inn's completion was a dream come true, and he couldn't hold back his excitement. The project was close to opening and having been more involved than ever meant Andy had a front row seat to everything that was happening—and those who were making it happen.

In the shots where he and Amanda were talking about design decisions, the producers thought they seemed more like a couple than Andy and Emma. They were giddy and finished each others' sentences. The chemistry was obvious, and Trudy and Rex made a decision to embrace it. For weeks they created all kinds of silly situations to have the two of them together on camera. They even captured them on their own when they thought nobody was watching.

Luann and Christy also earned extra "air time" when they started working together on projects. The producers hoped this relationship would develop into something more so they garnered more focus of the camera and crew—which didn't seem to phase either one of them. It made for good TV.

Lily embraced her Hawaiian heritage and dressed more and more like old Kauai royalty. She was the voice of those who couldn't speak and also those who could, and they were in her ear telling her to make the most of this opportunity (people of power on the island) and she listened. As a result, she was *treated* like royalty and invited to all the important local gatherings and meetings taking place... which she gladly accepted. As a result, Lily pushed for and got more ways to make it easier for locals to access and use the area.

Bradley was the reluctant television star. A handsome construction worker who looked like Thor in a tank top and jeans. He was something they could sell—but he wasn't buying. Bradley was all about the project and protecting Andy, so the only time he was on camera was when he was working or spending time with his friend.

The producers did their best to track Ray down using private investigators, but they struck out. A violent confrontation would be the best outcome, but a shouting match between Andy and Ray would do, too. Unfortunately, Ray was missing and nobody knew where he was.

Jim McDaniel found the time to be the Executive Producer he promised to be and vowed to oversee decisions about what made it into the final edits and ultimately on air. There were several serious discussions about what the show was about because they had captured such salacious material, but in the end everyone was able to hold their head high and know the show was a renovation show with some made-for-television moments that would captivate viewers and capture headlines. The show was destined to be a big hit based on the locale alone, but the behind-the-scenes antics and on-screen drama made it impossible to look away. The only question on the producer's minds was, would there be a season two?

CHAPTER 31

Ray knew better than anyone that this area of the island was haunted—that's why he played it up and tried to make Andy's "accidents" look like paranormal acts. So when Ray was on the run and woke up from a nightmare while sleeping under the cover of a canopy of trees not far from the inn, he was surprised to find his body covered with human bite marks—some that drew blood. To say he was freaked out did not cover his concern. Now he pondered turning himself in and coming clean. Maybe then the ghosts of his ancestors would leave him alone. Apparently these ghosts approved of what Andy was doing with their land and agreed with how he was using it to promote and recognize Hawaiian culture while helping others including locals deal with death.

The authorities surmised Ray was on his way to do the right thing and turn himself in at the Kapaa Police Station when his broken-down Toyota truck was rear-ended by tourists on the Kaumualii Highway, went out of control, and rolled into a ditch. Ray was pronounced dead at the scene. The tourists, an elderly couple from California, were uninjured. They claimed their rental car just stopped short all on its own. The driver swore he never touched the brakes—the car's data recorder confirmed the driver's account of the accident. It seemed like the spirits were appeased.

CHAPTER 32

"You know you didn't have to come all this way for the grand opening," Andy said to Jim and Lizzy McDaniel as the three sped along in a golf cart driven by Andy on their way to his newly-finished and furnished home.

"Seriously, you think I had anything better to do?" Jim asked rhetorically.

"Well, yeah. I'm sure you do. Aren't you two both starring in top-rated shows on television?"

"Nobody says television anymore, Andy. Get with the times," Jim pointed out.

"Sorry, you're both on some series about the old west that is a streaming success."

"Better," Jim joked.

"So Andy, where is the love of your life?" Lizzy wanted to know. Andy assumed she meant Emma and he stumbled over his answer.

Jim stepped in to save the day, as he always did. "Andy here is the proud owner of this very impressive property. I'm sure his focus is on making sure the first guests to arrive have a grand experience."

"Well, we are somewhere people come who have lost someone so my hope is their experience helps them better handle grief," Andy said, so proud of what was all around him.

"Everyone has lost someone, so I see big bucks," Jim said jokingly, but not joking.

"Jim, that's a terrible thing to say," Lizzy said and hit him lovingly, but forcefully on his chest.

"No, he's right. Unfortunately, we all have to deal with the loss of a loved one at some time in our lives," Andy aptly pointed out. "But for those who've lost a child, it's something worse and that's why we're here. To help them honor their loved ones while moving forward with their lives. It's not easy, trust me, I know, but it *is* possible."

It seemed like the whole world was on the island for the opening of Harper's Bay Inn and Retreat. It was partly because of the star power of Jim and Lizzy, combined with Andy and Emma's backstory, the wildly successful *Made Inn Hawaii* show, and the positively beautiful setting of it all that drew news crews from around the world.

The inn was already booked solid for the next few weeks and there was no telling what the tremendous publicity would generate going forward. In the end the goal was to help people with their grief and the booking process reflected that—to make a reservation you had to share your reason for wanting to stay there. There was a fund set up to offset the costs for families who couldn't afford it, and locals were able to stay for free. It wasn't a great business model, but it was what Andy wanted.

As they drove through the perfectly manicured grounds with the brand new buildings and facilities all shining in their glory, Andy was making mental notes as they went along of improvements and repairs he needed to make in the coming weeks to bring things up to his high standards.

Andy took Jim and Lizzy to his residence, a stand-alone, stilted home at the farthest corner of the property.

"I see you went with a Louisiana style structure for your own home, brother. I love it," Jim said as they drove up the elongated driveway. Another golf cart with the couple's luggage arrived at the same time.

"I had a lot of help with the design," Andy said, not willing to share the real reason he abandoned living in a one-bedroom bungalow on the beach for this much larger and grander abode, but he did mention the best feature as they walked up the steps to the wrap around balcony, "You can see the whole property from here."

The minute they all walked in Lizzy said, "Oh Andy, this is so you. Did you pick out the features and furnishings?"

"You probably think a country bumpkin like me doesn't have an eye for this kind of thing, do you?" Andy asked, not sure why he was so feisty.

"No. No I don't," Jim said with a smile.

"Fine! I found someone who gets me, loves me for who I am, and who also happens to be an interior designer. Okay?"

"No need to get snippy, Andy. Lizzy knows all about Amanda. Your lady friend even reached out before we got here to make sure we had everything we'd need for the perfect stay."

"Oh. I didn't know."

"Clearly."

"So where are you two staying?" Andy asked.

"We're in the main house and the kids and the band are in the bungalows," Jim replied.

"So our first guests are the whole McDaniel family?"

"Perfect, right?"

"Actually, yeah, it is."

"Are you ready for tonight's show?" Lizzy asked.

"No."

"Then I guess we should make sure we all make it to sound check on time," Jim replied.

"Right. I almost forgot I was playing tonight with all that's going on."

"Andy, it's your show and we're just here to help you shine."

"Of course that's what *you* would say. We both know this show is being filmed and that you two are the real reason people will watch it—sorry, stream it—when it comes out."

"That may be true, but I believe you and Harper are the real reasons everyone is here tonight, so let's give them the best show they've ever seen and let the chips fall where they may."

"What does that even mean, let the chips fall where they may."

"I don't know, Andy. It just sounded right."

Amanda pulled up in her golf cart and waved at the three recording stars standing on the lanai, not starstruck at all. The trade winds blew back her strawberry blonde hair and floral sundress as she bounded the steps to greet them.

"I'm Lizzy, it's so great to finally meet you in person," Lizzy said as she reached out to hug Amanda.

"Jim," was all the country star said as he held out a hand but instead gave her a hug. "Gotchu, didn't I?"

Amanda laughed, loving where life had taken her.

Andy was glowing with pride as he put his arm around Amanda and said, "See that over there, that's the stage they set up for us. Pretty cool, right?"

Jim asked, "Did anybody check the tides for tonight?"

Andy mocked hitting his forehead with his hand. "I didn't even think of that, but that's why I have Amanda."

"The tide is going out, nothing to worry about," Amanda replied.

For whatever reason, the talk of tides gave Andy a jolt and he was right back to the day Harper died. Amanda sensed it and squeezed his hand and said, "Why don't you tell Lizzy and Jim what they're looking at."

Andy pointed to the features of Harper's Bay Inn and Retreat. For the most part it was exactly how he drew it up during his stay in the hospital. However, building anything in Hawaii involved compromises.

Everything he wanted for the staff was built to plan. The water tower, and other environmentally-conscious endeavors all went off without a hitch.

The tree house and game room didn't end up in a tree, which was better because it was bigger—and air conditioned. That's not to say there weren't plenty of trees they could have built one in. Andy spent a fortune on foliage that serves to hide structures and creates the picture of paradise people expect.

The boat launch, beach hut, bar, ice cream and coffee shop were all exactly as he hoped they would be.

The restaurant was bigger and better than planned. The yoga and workout area were scaled back so the spa could be enlarged.

The beach bungalows were amazing and more were built than originally planned, but without Ray and Andy needing one and Luann and Lily opting to live off property, all the structures were for guests—except for Bradley's place, he decided to live in the end unit, by the newly added pool.

The Grief Center and Kauai cultural area were both expanded and exceptional.

Then there was the main house which was everything Andy ever wanted, and more.

In every space was a tribute to Harper of some kind. Only now instead of welling up when he saw them, Andy felt a sense of pride for the Harper he knew and loved and was grateful for the time he was in his life. Still, looking at the photos of when Harper was just a boy it seemed in some strange way like his eyes revealed he knew, he knew he wasn't going to live forever. It was haunting. And yet, Andy was coming to grips with the fact that Harper wasn't coming back. The life he knew with his son, his everything, was gone. He would never be whole again, but what helped him cope was his new routine.

Every morning Andy woke up with the sun and made the short walk from his home through the tree tunnel he helped plant to the grief center. He sat in the middle of the round room and pulled the photo of he and Harper from his dedicated drawer and began to talk his son, telling him what was happening in his life and how much he missed him. It didn't make everything better, but it helped.

EPILOGUE

One Year Later

Jim and Lizzy McDaniel encouraged Andy to move where the action was, Nashville. With the success of the reality show and his new album there was opportunity everywhere, but Andy's heart was where his home was, Kauai. Fame was not what Andy was after. His dream was to sing songs that touched people's hearts and build things that mattered. He was doing both. He did a short tour to support his debut album and was writing and recording when he had time. He was also very involved with the inn and most evenings put on a private show for the guests. For season two of *Made Inn Hawaii,* Andy and his team were rebuilding another inn on the other side of the island. He and Bradley worked side by side and he was able to wear a tool belt and get his hands dirty. Andy and Amanda were the stars of the show and their love story made for good television. Amanda served as the head designer for the project, even though she was six-months pregnant with twins.

Emma bought a brand new, turn-key estate situated on a man-made lake in a private gated community in Baton Rouge. Since she now lived alone, she indulged her own preference in real estate and decor—luxury all the way. She could afford it after opening her own law practice specializing in intellectual property law. She had a long list of famous and wealthy clients starting with Andy Clarke. Happiness still eluded her, but she buries herself in her work, dotes on her dog, is (mostly) sober, and hides her sorrow well.

Luann leased the space where Dani's Diner once was and opened her own eatery, "Lu Lu's". The place was an instant success and most mornings Andy was seated at the counter eating his breakfast. Bradley was hired to help with the restaurant's remodel, but Christy did it for free since she and Luann were now an item.

Lily invited Luann and Christy to live in her place in town and she moved into one of the bungalows on the beach at Harper's Bay. This way she could walk to work as the curator, guide, and director of the ever expanding Kauai Cultural Center next door to the inn. It turned out to be everything she hoped for, and more.

Made Inn Hawaii was such a hit Trudy was rewarded with a raise and promotion. She's now the sole producer of a new reality show on alligator hunters. The show is filmed on airboats in the Florida Everglades… in the middle of summer. This led Trudy to question many of her life choices. Rex refused the assignment and is working on a show about "drag" racing in Key West—kind of a Ru Paul meets *Driving Force*.

CAST OF CHARACTERS

Andy Clarke (Songwriter and Carpenter)
Emma Clarke (Attorney)
Harper Clarke (Deceased Son)
Ray (Raimanu) Collins (Hawaiian Handyman)
Luann "Lu" Kalama (Woman on Plane, Friend)
"Lily" (Lili'uokalani) Kalama (Luann's Aunt, Curator)
Jim McDaniel (Country Music Star and Investor)
Lizzy McDaniel (Country Music Star and Investor)
Bradley (Friend and Contractor from Slidell)
Trudy Thomas (Television Producer)
Randy "Tex" Tillerson (Television Producer)
Amanda Bennett (Interior Designer)
Clay (Handsome Helper)
Christy (Construction Worker)

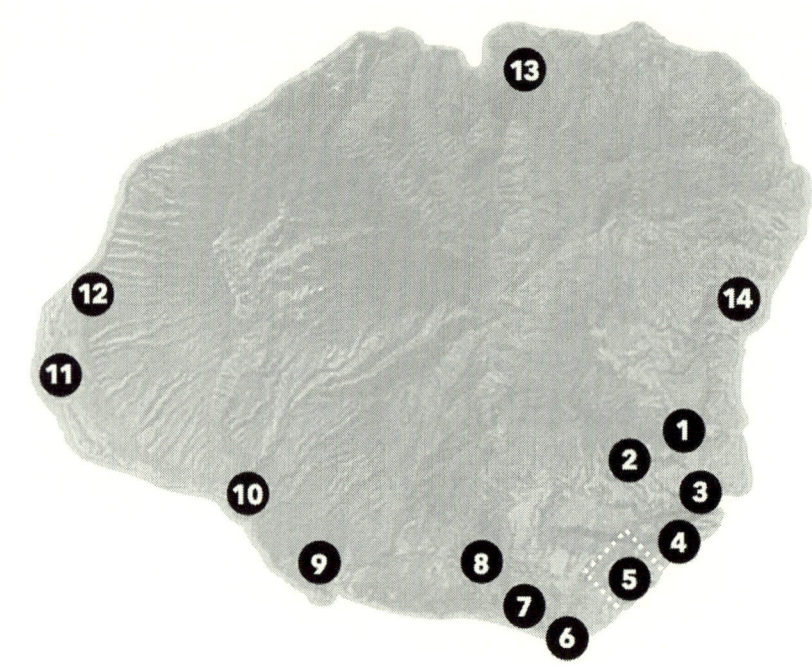

MAP OF THE ISLAND

1. **Lihue Airport** (30-minute Drive to Poipu)
2. **Lihue Town** (Home Depot, Hospital, Dani's)
3. **Kalapaki Beach** (Duke's, Nawiliwili Harbor)
4. **Kipu Kai Beach** (Nearby Secluded Beach and Bay)
5. **Harper's Bay Inn** (The Inn's 32 Acres of Land and Beach)
6. **Shipwreck Beach** (Where Harper Disappeared)
7. **Hyatt Resort** (Stevenson's Library)
8. **Poipu / Koloa** (Nearest Town, Keoki's, Fire Station)
9. **Hanapepe** (Quaint Artist Town)
10. **Waimea** (Plantation Cottages, Small Town)
11. **Barking Sands** (Pacific Missile Range, Shenanigans)
12. **Polihale State Park** (Large Beach)
13. **Princeville/Kilauea** (Where Celebrities Live)
14. **Kapaa** (Where Lily and Luann live)

THANK YOU

We all know you begin building a home by laying the foundation first, and then working your way up. Rebuilding a life is much the same, only the foundation isn't made up of brick and mortar. The material used in the foundation of a life is love. I know how schmaltzy that sounds, but I stand by it. Loving others, being loved, loving yourself, and loving what you do are the foundation of a good life. I'm fortunate to have the love and support of my soul mate who is the glue that holds everything together. For 26 books and 35 years my wife has helped me weather the storms and keep going.

Of all the things I have done, building a family and raising my sons has been my most important and rewarding endeavor. In this story, the loss of a child rips through the life of a husband and wife like a tornado and devastates everything and everyone in its path. I can only imagine (and I tried to for this book) what that would be like. It was unfathomable. As they grow up and move on it's a little like losing them, but that's life, right? I'm so proud of Ethan and Evan and who they've become. My goal is to make every moment with them count and to *never* have to write a song called "The Things I Wished I Said."

They say the key to success with any major construction

project is having a top-notch production manager to supervise and oversee everything. Andrew Chapman has been my publishing manager for over 20 years and has overseen dozens of my books—some we've written together. I wouldn't be where I am without him, so simply saying thank you isn't enough. So I will thank him in Hawaiian to drive the point home: *mahalo mai ko'u pu'uwai* (thank you from my heart).

Every one of my previous 25 books was edited by my mom. With her red pen at the ready she didn't miss a thing. This is the first book since her passing that she was not the first to read. What helped me the most was the support I received from other people along the way—early readers, reviewers, and editors like Julie Belmonte (an amazing author in her own right), Nanci Burg Canby, Ronald Collis (a guy who reads a book a day), Carole Elliot, Annie Gristina, Cristine Holmer, Carol White Horsely, Jason Mann, Bradley Steffens (a prolific and award-winning author), and especially Mary Valerio (who has been helping me for years with my books. Her input changed this book in a good way.) Thank you all. I love you guys—and any mistakes still in the book are totally my fault.

Lastly, if you enjoyed this book please post a review on Amazon, or write a nice note and send it through my website LeeSilber.com to "build" support for this book.

LYRICS

"The Things I Never Said"

You can't praise too much
Or love enough
When they're your heart and soul
Let them know

QUESTIONS

SPOILER ALERT!

The answers to the following questions give away aspects of the story. Skip to the next section if you haven't read the book yet.

I can only imagine the questions you have after reading this book. In fact, I did try to imagine what they would be so I could give you honest answers to each one. You can always reach out to me at leesilber@leesilber.com and I will answer any other questions you may have.

IS ANDY CLARKE'S CHARACTER BASED ON YOURSELF?

Not even close. If I was a tall, fit, handsome man from Louisiana who wrote a hit song, then yes. But I'm not. In my book, *The Pelican* I did make it personal, but for this novel I created characters that were very little like me—or anyone else I know.

DID YOU WATCH *RENOVATION ISLAND* ON HGTV?

Yes. I love that show. Did it influence the book? Not really. I already had the idea for the plot and characters of this book a long time ago. What the show did was make it seem like maybe others would be interested in a story like this. Fingers crossed, I hope so.

WHERE DID THE IDEA FOR THIS BOOK COME FROM?

Years ago my wife and I were struggling to have kids and we went to a fertility doctor. I knew the minute we walked into the doctor's office it was a bad idea, but my wife was convinced this doctor was the answer. After the consultation, the doctor mixed up the medicines and gave her the wrong shot. Instead of injecting her with a shot to increase her chances of getting pregnant, the injection she received was designed to prevent a person from getting pregnant... for a year. It also had some horrible side effects. We had already scheduled a trip to Kauai around this time, but once we got there my wife had to be hospitalized. She was out of it so when I wasn't by her side I was exploring Kauai. It was on a hike when I found Gillin's Beach. Just like in the book, there is a house in the middle of nowhere you can rent. At that time the beach was hard to get to by car, and not good for swimming, so it was empty. It was then that the beginnings of this book began to take shape. During this extended stay I really felt like a local. I always wanted to live on Kauai, but haven't made it happen... yet. So now I can live on Kauai vicariously through Andy.

WHAT PARTS ARE CLOSE TO REAL LIFE?

A lot, actually. Hopefully, if you've ever been to Kauai (or better yet, live there) a lot of this story will ring true. Little Fish Coffee, Kalapaki Joe's, Keoki's, Duke's, and Stevenson's Library and the Grand Hyatt Resort and Spa are all real—and real good. Dani's was a real restaurant on Rice Street in Lihue that locals loved. Me, too. It closed, but reopened as Kauai Diner. Ship-wreck Beach is also a real place—and so is the nearby cliff people jump from. Yes, a few have died from jumping off, just not exactly like how I described Harper's demise—but close. The day trip to Polihale the girl's take is the same as my favorite day of any Kauai trip. The base (and Shenanigan's) is real, but the only time we were able to get on was for a Fourth of July celebration. The Waimea Plantation Cottages are such a cool place they are also the focus of my first novel, *Runaway Best Seller*. I l-o-v-e that place. Kipu Kai Beach, real. The Mahaulepu trail is also real, as are the hauntings. Apparently, a fisherman fell asleep on the trail and awoke from a nightmare to find human bite marks all over his body. Oh, and yes, Drew Brees does live part time on Kauai with a home near Princeville and neighbors that include Ben Stiller, Carlos Santana, and others.

WHY SLIDELL?

I love New Orleans and I have been there several times to speak at conferences. However, crossing the long bridge across Lake Pontchartrain is like going to another world. On one of my speaking tours I met a mother and daughter who took me in and I swear for the few days I was in Slidell I felt a part of their family. That's never happened anywhere else. They also "insisted" I eat gator and do shots of moonshine—it was a memorable trip. Obviously, it stuck with me enough to make it into this book.

WHY IS THERE A SEAPLANE ON THE COVER?

The seaplane is a nod to Jimmy Buffett who owned and piloted a 1954 Grumman Albatross. When he died in the summer of 2023, I took it really hard. Not because we were close friends—

we had met—but because I was a such a big fan. I liked his music, but loved his backstory. He was someone who by his own admission was not the best singer or guitar player. Instead, he focused on his strengths (songwriting and performing). His first album sold less than 500 copies and he was dropped by his record label, but throughout his career he overcame setbacks and struggles with hard work and by charging forward. Buffett built a business empire around one song and a t-shirt shop by the same name on Duval Street in Key West—*Margaritaville*. When he didn't get any airplay and his career was in decline, Jimmy wrote a best selling book, built a recording studio, released his albums on his own label, and was one of the first to have an internet-only radio station. He also wrote plays, appeared as an actor in movies and television, and was an active conservationist. For those and other reasons Jimmy Buffett was and is my role model. I wanted to honor him for how much he inspired me to chase *my* dreams and thought the plane was the way to do it—plus Andy Clarke's character has a little bit of Jimmy Buffett in *his* backstory.

DID YOU KNOW HOW IT WOULD END ALL ALONG?

"Kill your babies." That's what my literary agent once told me. I interpreted that as someone has to die. In past books, it was easy to see whose demise was inevitable. Here, not so much. Oh, I killed them all off at one point or another in my head, but it didn't feel right. Besides, I love a happy ending. (Sorry, but I also sometimes watch the Hallmark channel.) In the end I decided Ray would have to go, but that wasn't enough. More tragedy and heartache was needed. I was talking to a friend of mine about my dilemma and as someone who tragically lost two children, he mentioned it was impossible to sit and have dinner with his ex-wife and not feel sad, so they split up. In a way I was relieved I didn't have to kill anyone else off, but it pained me that Andy and Emma wouldn't make it as a couple. As someone who has been with the same person for over 30 years, I was rooting for a reunion. And yet, I think the characters were better served by being apart.

MORE BOOKS

RUNAWAY BEST SELLER

Sometimes escaping can be the most dangerous thing to do.

All Kate Ramirez wanted to do was leave her lying, cheating, abusive husband behind and start a new life in a tropical paradise. But that's not so easy to do when he's a well-known pro baseball player being prosecuted for your murder and you unexpectedly become a best-selling author. Suddenly your new, quiet life in the tropics gets very complicated—and extremely dangerous.

Available from Amazon in paperback and Kindle

THE HOMELESS HERO

In this case, a daughter can save her father and save the day.

Thomas "Big Mac" MacDonald lost everything in the divorce—his home, his National Football League pension, and his dignity—everything but his prized, classic, VW van. It would be enough to drive anyone to drink, but that's only the half of it. The "residents" of the beach park where Thomas and dozens of other homeless San Diegans sleep in their cars are suddenly disappearing at a rapid rate. With the help of his twelve-year-old daughter, Big Mac begins rebuilding his life, and solving the mystery at the same time.

Available from Amazon in paperback and Kindle (approved for all ages)

SUNSHINE

They say some people have all the fun—Sunshine Blake was one of those people.

When Sunshine was a teenager she made a promise to herself to see the world and live a glamorous life. Nobody believed she could do it. Why would they? She was abused and abandoned by her parents and shuffled from foster home to foster home in the poorest part of the country. Yet Sunshine accomplished everything she set out to do—and then some. Sunshine's extraordinary life was a wild and exciting ride with twists and turns, ups and downs, and adventures all over the globe. Sunshine's incredible life story can change yours.

Available from Amazon in paperback and Kindle

THE SPLENDID SPLINTER

Doc Skinner loved his players, his boat, and his life—now all three are in jeopardy.

When Doc Skinner retired as the longtime hitting coach for the San Diego Padres he lived a simple life aboard his boat at the Island Marina. Taylor Livingston, one of his former (and favorite) players was in a cabin cruiser across the way, and the daughter of his closest friend stayed in a sailboat two slips over. When Doc and his boat suddenly disappear out of the blue, it's all hands on deck as the cast of characters from the marina search for their missing friend.

Available from Amazon in paperback and Kindle

◈ ◈ ◈

JIMMY AND THE KID

When a twelve-year-old girl wants to play baseball with the boys, she's lucky to have the help of a former Major Leaguer with the power to change her life forever.

Escaping to the empty baseball fields across the street from the military housing in which she lives, Billie is content to throw a ball against the wall, pitching imaginary games with no one around—until she meets Jimmy Parks, the man who maintains the fields. Not only does the long-retired Major Leaguer teach Billie and her new friends how to play baseball the right way, he and the other older coaches also teach the team about life in this story of breaking barriers—and breaking through to do what you were always meant to do.

Available from Amazon in paperback and Kindle

◈ ◈ ◈

UNDERGROUND

One underground fort, two teenagers, and three hours to save two undercover agents. Can they do it?

This is a teen thriller approved for all ages. As a teenager who didn't dream of having their own place to go where they could lock the door, do what they want, and nobody would know? What started out as a special place to hide out became the one safe place in a young boy's life—until he confides in his best friend, neighbor, and the love of his life about the abduction of his dad, a DEA Agent. This leads the two on a manhunt that has them punching above their weight and rising to the challenge every step of the way.

Available free at LeeSilber.com/resources-mini

THE AUTHOR

.

LEE SILBER is the award-winning author of 25 books. For many of his previous titles he went to great lengths to research the characters in his books including living on the streets of San Diego, spending the final weeks with a dying friend, doing odd jobs and going undercover in companies, and spending a month on Kauai to write *Runaway Best Seller*. For this book, Lee took on several home improvement projects for himself and others to get in touch with his inner handyman—and he went to Hawaii to research the locations in the book. Silber is also a motivational speaker and corporate trainer. For a list of his topics and to learn more go to: www.leesilber.com. Lee and his family live in Mission Beach, California.

Made in the USA
Middletown, DE
17 October 2025

19271045R00111